'unchy and entertaining . . . Johnson is adept at cryptic
l; the prose is full of snappy lines and withering
racterisations'   ***Daily Telegraph***

lean, rough, dizzying amoral noir thriller about a couple
bad apples on the run from a couple of worse ones'
Time

mson is a fine novelist and a good poet. In this thriller
s really enjoying himself, and it shows on every page'
Daily Mail

blackly comic crime tale, with a wicked sense of fun'
Washington Post

neo-noir Western that summons Dashiell Hammett
d Cormac McCarthy. Terrific stuff'   ***GQ***

'mson's sex-fuelled noir novel packs white heat'
Vanity Fair

olayful, noirish, high-wire crime caper set in California,
h style always at the service of narrative and Johnson's
quivocal authorial vision ensuring ambiguity is in as
rt supply as love, mercy and compassion'   ***Metro***

.gely enjoyable and fast-moving . . . A flinty piece of
pop art meant to be instantly understood and enjoyed'
New York Times

'*Nobody Move* – the title may well be a stage direction for the reader as well as the assorted characters, most of whom are operating on the wrong side of the law. This is a staccato romp, as violent as Tarantino and a great deal funnier than Cormac McCarthy'   *Irish Times*

'A hard-boiled, modern shoot-'em-up in which nobody's hands are clean but everyone gets great lines' *USA Today*

'Johnson brings his own idiosyncratic brilliance, an ear for off-beat dialogue as good as Elmore Leonard's and a well-practised gift for poet dislocation to its tough, racy narrative. And beyond its ferocious action, noisy gun-play and relentless wisecracking is an understanding of a bleak, inhospitable world'   *Uncut*

'Short, sharp and written in the snappy prose of which Elmore Leonard is the master and Denis Johnson the number one disciple'   *Books Quarterly*

'The adventures come thick and fast, as do the wisecracking baddies and sexy, dangerous, kooky women' *City A.M.*

'Denis Johnson's novel features a couple of testicle-eating bad guys, a femme fatale with a stake in several million missing dollars, and a skinny-chested teetotal gambler who tumbles downstairs as readily as he falls into bad situations; all this involving guns, box cutters, shovels, women and other dangerous implements'   *TLS*

NOBODY MOVE

DENIS JOHNSON is the author of six previous novels,
a collection of poetry, and one book of reportage.
His most recent novel, *Tree of Smoke*, won the
2007 US National Book Award. He lives in
northern Idaho.

ALSO BY DENIS JOHNSON

DENIS JOHNSON

NOBODY MOVE

PICADOR

First published 2009 by Farrar, Straus and Giroux, New York

First published in Great Britain 2009 by Picador

This edition published 2010 by Picador
an imprint of Pan Macmillan, a division of Macmillan Publishers Limited
Pan Macmillan, 20 New Wharf Road, London N1 9RR
Basingstoke and Oxford
Associated companies throughout the world
www.panmacmillan.com

ISBN 978-0-330-50402-7

A CIP catalogue record for this book is available from
the British Library.

Printed in the UK by CPI Mackays, Chatham ME5 8TD

for Meir Ribalow

PART ONE

PART ONE

PART ONE

JIMMY LUNTZ had never been to war, but this was the sensation, he was sure of that—eighteen guys in a room, Rob, the director, sending them out—eighteen guys shoulder to shoulder, moving out on the orders of their leader to do what they've been training day and night to do. Waiting silently in darkness behind the heavy curtain while on the other side of it the MC tells a stale joke, and then—"THE ALHAMBRA CALIFORNIA BEACH-COMBER CHORDSMEN!"—and they were smiling at hot lights, doing their two numbers.

Luntz was one of four leads. On "Firefly" he thought they did pretty well. Their vowels matched, they went easy on the consonants, and Luntz knew he, at least, was lit up and smiling, with plenty of body language. On "If We Can't Be the Same Old Sweethearts" they caught the wave. Uniformity, resonance, expression of pathos, everything Rob had ever asked for. They'd never done it so well. Right face, down the steps, and into the convention center's basement, where once again they arranged themselves in ranks, this time to pose for souvenir pictures.

"Even if we come in twentieth out of twenty," Rob told them afterward, while they were changing out of their gear, the white tuxedos and checkered vests and checkered bow ties, "we're really coming in twentieth out of a hundred, right? Because remember, guys, one hundred outfits tried to get to this competition, and only twenty made it all the way here to Bakersfield. Don't forget that. We're out of a hundred, not twenty. Remember that, okay?" You got a bit of an impression Rob didn't think they'd done too well.

Almost noon. Luntz didn't bother changing into street clothes. He grabbed his gym bag, promised to meet the others back at the Best Value Inn, and hurried upstairs still wearing the getup. He felt the itch to make a bet. Felt lucky. He had a Santa Anita sheet folded up in the pocket of his blinding white tux. They started running at twelve-thirty. Find a pay phone and give somebody a jingle.

On his way out through the lobby he saw they'd already posted the judgments. The Alhambra Chordsmen ranked seventeenth out of twenty. But, come on, that was really seventeenth out of a hundred, right?

All right—fine. They'd tanked. But Luntz still had that lucky feeling. A shave, a haircut, a tuxedo. He was practically Monte Carlo.

He headed out through the big glass doors, and there's old Gambol standing just outside the entrance. Checking the comings and goings. A tall, sad man in expensive slacks and shoes, camel-hair sports coat, one of those white straw hats that senior-citizen golfers wear. A very large head.

"So hey," Gambol said, "you are in a barbershop chorus."

"What are you doing here?"

"I came here to see you."

"No, but really."

"Really. Believe it."

"All the way to Bakersfield?"

That lucky feeling. It had let him down before.

"I'm parked over here," Gambol said.

Gambol was driving a copper-colored Cadillac Brougham with soft white leather seats. "There's a button on the side of the seat," he said, "to adjust it how you want."

"People will be missing me," Luntz said. "I've got a ride back down to LA. It's all arranged."

"Call somebody."

"Good, sure—just find a pay phone, and I'll hop out."

Gambol handed him a cell phone. "Nobody's hopping anywhere."

Luntz patted his pockets, found his notebook, spread it on his knee, punched buttons with his thumb. He got Rob's voice mail and said, "Hey, I'm all set. I got a lift, a lift back down to Alhambra." He thought a second. "This is Jimmy." What else? "Luntz." What else? Nothing. "Good deal. I'll see you Tuesday. Practice is Tuesday, right? Yeah. Tuesday."

He handed back the phone, and Gambol put it in the pocket of his fancy Italian sports coat.

Luntz said, "Okay if I smoke?"

"Sure. In your car. But not in my car."

•

Gambol drove with one hand on the wheel and one long arm reaching into the back seat, going through Luntz's gym bag. "What's this?"

"Protection."

"From what? Grizzly bears?" He reached across Luntz's lap and shoved it in the glove compartment. "That is one big gun."

Luntz opened the compartment.

"Shut that thing, goddamn it."

Luntz shut it.

"You want protection? Pay your debts. That's the best protection."

"I agree completely," Luntz said, "and can I tell you about an uncle of mine? I have an appointment to see him this afternoon."

"A rich uncle."

"Coincidentally, yes. He just moved out from the coast. Made a pile in the garbage business. The guy gets a new Mercedes every year. Just moved to Bakersfield. Last time I saw him he was still living in La Mirada. The Garbage King of La Mirada. Told me anytime I needed money to get in touch. We had lunch at the Outback Steakhouse in La Mirada. Wow, do they deliver. Choice cuts as thick as your arm. You ever try the Outback?"

"Not lately."

"So, in other words, let me give this guy a call before we get too far out of town."

"In other words, you can't make a payment."

"Yes, definitely, yes," Luntz said, "I can make a payment. Just let me use your phone and work a little magic."

Gambol behaved as if he hadn't heard.

"Come on. The guy drives a Mercedes. Let me go see him."

"Fucking bullshit. Your uncle."

"Okay. He's Shelly's uncle. But he's real."

"Is Shelly real?"

"She's—yeah. Shelly? I used to live with her."

"The uncle of some bitch you used to live with."

"Give me a chance, friend. A chance to work my magic."

"You're working it now. It ain't working."

"Look, man, look," Luntz said, "let's call Juarez. Let me talk to the man himself."

"Juarez is not a talker."

"Come on. Don't we know each other? What's the problem?"

Gambol said, "My brother just died."

"What?"

"He died exactly a week ago."

Luntz knew nothing about any brother. How do you

reason with someone who throws something like that into the conversation?

They were heading north. Bakersfield stank of oil and natural gas. In the most unlikely places, in the middle of a shopping mall or next to one of those fancy new churches, all glass and swooping curves, you'd see oil rigs with their heads going up and down.

•

"Used to fish up here with my brother," Gambol said, "somewhere around here anyway. On the Feather River."

Luntz unclasped his hands from each other and looked at them. "What?"

"Once, to be exact. We went fishing one time. We should've done it more."

The road was a four-lane, but not an interstate. The clock on the dash said 4:00 p.m.

"Where are we?"

"We're just driving around," Gambol said. "Why? You need to be someplace?"

Luntz placed his hands on his knees and sat up straight. "Where are we going?"

"On this kind of trip, you don't want to ask where it ends."

Luntz closed his eyes.

When he opened them he saw a crowd of bikers on Harleys coming toward them and sweeping past.

Gambol said, "See that? Half those bikies had Oregon plates. I think there's a convention in Oakland or someplace like that. Guess what? I've never been on a motorcycle."

"Shit," Luntz said.

"What?"

"Nothing. Those bikers. Shit," he said, "the Feather River. Is there a Feather River Tavern or something?"

"The river's not anywhere around here. It's more north. Guess what? You'll never get me on a Harley."

"Yeah?"

"Helmet or not. What good is a helmet?"

"The Feather fucking River," Luntz said.

•

Standing at the pay phone, Jimmy Luntz punched a nine and a one and stopped. He couldn't hear the dial tone. His ears still rang. That old Colt revolver made a bang that slapped you silly.

He dropped the receiver and let it dangle a few seconds. He shook his head and wiped both hands across the thighs of his slacks. He jabbed at the one again as he put the phone to his head. Some woman said, "Palo County Sheriff's Department. What is your emergency?"

"A guy. This guy," he said. "A guy's been shot."

"What is your name and location, sir?"

"Well, we're at this rest stop north of the Tastee-Freez on Seventy, somewhere past Ortonville. Way past Ortonville."

"Sir. Do you mean Oroville?"

"On the nose," he said. He searched with his free hand for a cigarette.

"Do you see a milepost marker, sir?"

"No. There's these big pines right by the road. Kind of behind there."

"The rest stop north of the Tastee-Freez and north of Oroville. What's his condition, can you tell me?"

Luntz said, "He got shot in the leg. How do you make a tourniquet?"

"Just apply direct pressure to the wound. Is he conscious?"

"He's fine, honey. But the blood's just pouring."

"Apply pressure. Put a clean cloth down and press hard on the wound with the palm of your hand."

"I'll do that, yeah, but I mean—can you get here pretty quick?"

She started talking again, and he hung up.

He found his lighter and got his Camel going. Took several deep puffs, threw it aside.

He went across the rest stop under the evergreens to where Gambol sat propped against the left rear wheel of his Cadillac, looking very pale. Very large. He'd removed his white golfing hat. What a head. A huge head. His entire right pants leg was soaked black with blood. The white hat lay beside him.

Luntz bent from his waist and unbuckled Gambol's belt, and Gambol opened his big foreign-looking eyes.

Luntz said, "I need your belt for a tourniquet."

He put his foot between the man's big legs and dragged the belt free through the loops around his fat middle. "Look, brother," he said to Gambol, "I hope you understand."

Gambol breathed deep a couple times but didn't seem able to speak.

Luntz said, "Am I supposed to sit around and wait for you to break my arm? When was the last time you got a broken bone?"

Gambol huffed and puffed. He felt for his hat beside him, brought it to his chest, and held it there. "Guess what?" he managed to say. "I got a busted thigh bone right this minute."

"I called 911, so just hang on."

With surprising energy, Gambol suddenly tossed away his white hat. The wind caught it, and it sailed a dozen yards into the trees. Then he seemed to lose consciousness.

Luntz dropped the belt in Gambol's bloody lap. He parted the lapels of Gambol's camel-hair sports coat and reached inside for Gambol's wallet and pocketed it.

He hiked his slacks and squatted and felt under the car where the old gun had ended up, found the thing, and stood up straight, gripping the gun with both hands. He placed the muzzle against Gambol's forehead and rested one thumb on the hammer.

Gambol seemed oblivious. His hands lay open either side of his outstretched legs, and his belly went up and down.

Luntz took his thumb from the hammer and let out his breath and lowered the gun. "Fuck. Put that around your leg. The belt, man. Wake up, man." Gambol's face was like a stupid child's as he grasped an end of the belt with each hand to drag it up under his bloody leg. "Through the buckle there, the buckle," Luntz said. "It's a tourniquet," he said as he got in the car.

He settled himself into the Caddy's white leather. He turned the key. He lowered the window and called out, "You better move, Gambol, because this Caddy's about to roll."

He yanked the stick into drive and floored it out of the parking lot and, at the highway's entrance, slammed the brake hard.

They'd be coming from the south, he guessed, from the hospital in Ortonville, Oroville, wherever. He turned north.

After he passed a highway patrol car heading toward him fast, lights whirling, he simply couldn't drive any farther and hooked into a café's parking lot on the outskirts of a town.

He put the Caddy behind the building and wiped his face with his sleeve. Sweat soaked his shirt and vest. He touched the dials of the climate control tenderly, stupidly, couldn't make sense of them. Got out and removed the jacket and tie and vest and stood in the breeze, grabbed the doorframe, and bent double and vomited sour green liquid between his black shoes.

In the men's room Luntz stood at the urinal a full minute, but nothing came out of him. He flushed anyway.

He put his hands on the sink and bowed his head and breathed several times in and out before raising his eyes to the mirror.

•

Around 11:00 a.m. Anita Desilvera went to the movies with a half pint of Popov vodka in her purse. As she approached the building she caught a glimpse of the poster for this epic: *The Last Real Champ.*

She bought a ticket from the stone-faced man in the box and went inside. She purchased a large pink lemonade, and on her way into the auditorium she dumped half of it into the drinking fountain with a clatter of ice cubes. Made her way down the aisle in the dark to one of the front rows. She sat down leaving her coat on and bowed her face against the seat in front of her for several seconds, then raised it up weeping.

Opened the bottle and poured the vodka into her drink, kicked the empty under the next seat.

This movie appeared to be about prizefighters. Gigantic boxing gloves plowed great globs of sweat from foreheads and jowls in extreme close-up. A man alone two rows ahead of her jerked and grunted as he followed the action: "Huh! Hah! Hoh!"

While men on the screen beat each other's faces to pieces she sat in the dark and got thirty percent drunk and found a kerchief in the pocket of her overcoat and buried her face in it and wept with greater abandon. There was really no other place for the wife of the Palo County prosecutor to gulp down booze and grieve. She didn't even have a key to her own house. They'd taken everything but the car.

When her watch said ten minutes till noon she made her way to the washroom and got her face back together and ran a brush through her hair and went out to the glaring street.

The Packard Room lay two blocks from the theater. She walked briskly and breathed deeply. Outside the place she smoothed her gray skirt and straightened her coat, and as she entered the cool light of the greenhouse dining room she kept her shoulders back and made sure to smile with her entire face.

Hank Desilvera sat over in the corner looking rich. He smiled back at her like the Prince of All Tomorrow while dipping to get papers from his briefcase.

By the time she'd draped her coat on the empty chair and sat herself down, the meanest meal of her life lay at her place: The plea agreement. The letter of resignation. The waiver. Three copies of each.

She picked up the pen and signed. Flushing her life away took forty-five seconds.

Hank just laughed and put the stuff back in his briefcase beside his chair. He shrugged. He managed to make all this seem like a tough loss for her in what was sure to be an otherwise glorious season.

He could fuck you, frame you, and roll you onto the street—and expect you to be having fun.

"Tanneau has the rest of it," he said. Tanneau was the judge. The rest of it was the divorce papers.

"Hank," she said, "can't we work on this? We can work this out. Look," she said, "I know how to forgive. I believe in forgiveness." She'd intended to sit all the way through this lunch, display a little style, but two minutes into it she'd already made herself a beggar.

"Not every day comes out symmetrical, Babylove."

"Don't ever call me that."

"Babylove," he said, and the word went right down through her. "What about the Cajun chicken?"

"What?"

"It's new."

"New?"

"Yeah. Try the Cajun chicken."

"I'd love to! But I've got a conflict." She was already getting her coat on. "Will you mail me my copies?"

"Where to?" he said.

"Where to?"

"What's the address? Where do you live life these days?"

She stood staring at him while they both realized she had absolutely no answer to the question.

"And where are you off to at the moment?"

"I've got an appointment with the judge."

"The judge is out," Hank said.

"I've got an appointment." She grabbed up the papers and stuffed them in the pocket of her coat and left.

Tanneau had his offices in a renovated brick building, formerly a power station, now a high-rent fortress of commerce and law. He owned it. Despite all the vodka, the idea of seeing him had her heart pounding as she walked in the sunshine, in the aroma of evergreens, in all these atmospheres covering the stench. She would take the stairs, she would announce herself, she'd be ushered into the aura of his greatness, and he'd stand politely while she seated herself before his desk. He'd take his place behind it, fold his hands, lean toward her, and stare at her in mild confusion and sorrow, as if he couldn't think of any reason why she'd come. He looked like a TV preacher with his big white coif, sentimental and telegenic. It could only have been a matter of time before he and Hank Desilvera had rubbed together and caught fire and started burning anybody fool enough to get close to either of them. And she'd gotten close to both: secretary to the judge, wife of the county prosecutor.

When she got to Tanneau's office, the brand-new secretary claimed he wasn't in. "I'm sorry—did you have an appointment?"

"He needed a signature."

But this new secretary, Anita's replacement, a middle-aged woman in a chestnut frock, found nothing in the files for Anita Desilverio.

"Desilver-*a*. For Jesus' sake. Mrs. Henry Desilvera? The divorce agreement?"

"Oh. God. Yes," her replacement said.

She had the copies in her in-basket. Anita signed all three and kept one. "Allow me." She dropped two copies in the basket marked OUT. Six months from now—that would be that. In a single morning with some documents and a little ink she'd made herself a vagrant, a felon, and a future divorcee.

She turned and slapped the judge's door three times with the flat of her hand. "You know I'm out here."

Her replacement drew a quick breath. "I told you—the judge isn't in."

Anita put both her hands flat against the door. She laid her cheek against its wood. "EIGHT HUNDRED BUCKS A MONTH. FOREVER."

Her replacement reached for the phone.

"If I have to pay restitution for the rest of my life, guess what? You can expect to hear me yell."

"Yell outside, then. The judge isn't in there. He's in the hospital."

"Really?"

"He went for a biopsy Friday, and they took him right into surgery."

"I hope he dies."

"You're drunk."

"Not yet. But I like the way you think."

•

Gambol permitted himself to rest on his back on the tarmac for one minute, checking this interval by his wristwatch, and then rolled himself over onto his belly and put his palms flat against the pavement either side of his shoulders. He rested thirty seconds before he raised himself to crawl forward on two hands and one knee, head hanging, taking ragged breaths, hauling his wounded leg toward the protection of the pines.

Propped against a tree trunk, he rested for two minutes. When he opened his eyes the branches overhead seemed to be rushing away into the sky.

He got his cell phone in his hand and punched Juarez on the speed dial.

"Yowsah. Mistah Gambolino."

"I need a doctor."

"So get a doctor."

"I need a friendly doctor. I'm shot, man."

"Shot?"

"That fucking Jimmy Luntz."

"What?"

"Jimmy Luntz shot me."

"What?"

"I need a doctor. And I need a ride. I need him to come and get me. I need a ride."

"You hurt bad? You can't drive?"

"The fucker took my car."

"What?"

"Fuck 'what.' He shot me through my leg. My right thigh. Through the bone, I think."

"Your thigh?"

"I got out to open the trunk, and he—bang, man."

"Where are you?"

"Oh, man."

"Gambol, stay with me. Where are you?"

"I'm near Oroville."

"Where's Ortonville? You in San Diego County or something?"

"Not Ortonville, man. Oroville. It's on Route Seventy. Way the hell up here past Sacramento and all that."

"Which direction from Oroville? Like east, west, what?"

"I think north."

"North. Near Madrona? I got a friend in Madrona."

"Get me the fuck out of here."

"I'm on it. Where did he shoot you?"

"In the *thigh*. I *told* you."

"Luntz?"

"Luntz."

"Jimmy Luntz? Oh, fuck. Oh, fuck. He will die. My promise to you."

"You bet your ass."

"My promise and my gift to you. He's dead."

Gambol shut his phone and dropped it into his breast

pocket. He paused for half a minute before undertaking the effort of tightening the belt around his leg. The leg was numb, and he felt cold.

He laid his head back against the tree trunk and considered the movements to follow and reviewed his consideration carefully before letting himself tip rightward onto his elbow and wrestling himself, by stages, onto his belly. As he stiffened his arms, raised himself, and began crawling forward, the phone fell from his pocket, and he stopped. He went down onto his elbows and took hold of it with his mouth.

Gripping his bloody cell phone in his teeth he dragged himself several yards farther into the pines and scrub and lay on his belly while sirens approached and arrived.

When he heard voices getting near he struggled onto his side and saw the ambulance not far beyond the point where he'd entered the small stand of pines, and three paramedics talking with two uniformed cops, cursing and laughing. The patrolmen had parked their cruiser right over the large stain on the blacktop. Even from this distance Gambol could make out his own blood trail.

He turned onto his back, buttoned his cell phone into his jacket's lapel pocket, and worked himself into position and dragged his leg farther away from the parking lot and lay in the mouth of a concrete culvert, where he waited, staring straight upward, blinking rapidly to keep himself conscious, while the two crews decided they'd been lured here as some kind of prank.

The crews didn't stay long. As they passed over the culvert he heard their vehicles thumping on the highway above his head.

He had difficulty unbuttoning the inner pocket of his jacket and further difficulty working the buttons on his phone. He reached Juarez again. "Did you find somebody?"

"I'm close. Stay with me. I think we can get you out of there. I know a vet in Madrona."

"I'm down in a culvert. I can't move my legs."

"Jesus, man, call an ambulance."

"Luntz called already. They came and went."

"Call them back!"

"Piss on that shit."

"Will you just call them back?"

"I'm at the end of the blacktop, in some trees."

"Tell me again—Route 70."

"The rest stop by the Tastee-Freez north of Oroville."

"I'm writing it down."

"I'm in a culvert under the road. You got that?"

"Keep that phone by you."

"It's right here. Send somebody."

"I'll try. But what if I can't?"

"Then eat that fucker's liver while he watches."

"It's a promise."

Gambol closed the phone.

He managed to sit upright against the side of the culvert. The breeze coming through it felt icy. Vehicles rumbled overhead. He laid his cell phone in his lap and tore at his bloody pants leg and got a look at the purple lipless exploded mouth in his flesh. He cinched the belt as tightly as it would go, but his hands were asleep and the wound seemed to well up and spill over, suck back, well up, spill over in a small but relentless way.

The phone rang. He got his fingers around it and raised it to his cheek. Juarez said, "I told you I knew somebody. I'm sending a vet."

Gambol opened his lips. Nothing came out.

"You there?"

"Yeah."

"I found you a vet. Thirty minutes. Stay put, now, hear? Don't run off."

Gambol failed to laugh. He tried saying, "Yeah," one more time, but his lips didn't move.

He dozed, woke, had no idea how much time had passed, saw that a rivulet of his blood traveled away from him, moving over the dirt collected in the groove of the culvert, disappearing again under massed brown pine needles. He raised his hand to look at his watch but couldn't get it up to his face.

"Hey—" he said, but very faintly. He himself could hardly hear it.

He put his fingers around the phone in his lap. The phone slipped away with a clatter that echoed in the concrete cylinder, and he let himself collapse toward it. He had his mouth by the phone. He had a finger on the button. He needed the finger to press it. He couldn't make it happen.

No problem. If he could keep his eyes open, he wasn't dead. Lying on his belly he stared at the red spectacle of his life as it traveled past his face and headed away from him through the dust. That's all he needed to do now. He needed to keep seeing his blood.

•

In the café Luntz sat quite still with his elbows on the counter and a menu in his face.

"Are you going to order?" the waitress asked.

"Is there a Feather River Tavern around here?"

"I don't know."

"Feather River Café, something like that?"

"I don't think so. Are you going to order?"

"Ice tea," he said, and took a second trip to the men's room.

He washed his hands and splashed his face with cold water and dried himself with hot air from a nozzle. He smoked half a cigarette in several rapid puffs and threw the rest in the toilet, went out the door, and lifted the receiver of the pay phone beside the restrooms.

Shelly answered and accepted the charges.

"Hey. It's me," he said.

"What's this collect?" Shelly said. "Are you someplace weird?"

"I'm near Oroville."

He heard her sigh.

"Listen. Shelly, listen. I got on a very messed-up ride with this guy I sort of know. A guy who intended to hurt me. And I think some people are probably coming to see you, Shelly. In fact, I'd count on it. Yeah."

"You mean cops?"

"Just people."

"People?"

"It's bad."

"Jimmy, Jesus Christ, Oroville? What's Oroville? What happened?"

"I wish I knew."

"You don't *know*?"

"I wish I could tell you. But if anybody wants me— just tell them you heard from me, I'm long gone, I'm never coming back."

He heard her breath in his ear, nothing else.

"Shelly, it's a mess. I'm sorry."

"Well, sorry fixes everything, don't it?"

"You gotta be mad as all get-out."

"Yeah, pretty much."

"I'm sorry, buddy," he said, and hung up.

"How much for the tea?" he asked the waitress as he sat down again.

"One fifty. Aren't you going to drink it?"

"Let me have a pack of Camel straights, please."

Gambol's wallet was so fat Luntz had to stand up to pry it out of his front pants pocket. Fat mostly with hundreds. He found a twenty.

"There might be a Feather River Inn," she said. "Kind of way up on the Feather River Road."

Luntz put the wallet away. "No longer an issue," he said.

•

Luntz sat in the car in the café's parking lot listening to an AM sports talk show and counting his blessings: forty-three one-hundred-dollar bills and change, plus a wallet with a tab inside it that said "Genuine Calfskin," and lots of credit cards. The cards had to go. And probably the car. And definitely the gun.

In his trembling hands he fanned out the crisp new Franklins. It wasn't much more than this that he owed Juarez in the first place.

Before he took off he cracked the Caddy's trunk to see what else Gambol might have bequeathed him. Popped the lid and found a heavy white canvas duffel in there and unzipped it.

The duffel held a shiny chrome-barreled pistol-grip shotgun and five, six—seven small boxes labeled "00 Buck," with maybe eight or ten to a box.

A pale green squad car cruised the far edge of the parking lot. A county rig. Luntz zipped the bag and closed the trunk.

•

First town he hit he bought a fifty-dollar phone card at the Safeway and called information at the pay phone out front. "Alhambra, California. Dooley's Tavern. No. Wait a minute. Dooley's is like a nickname. It's O'Doul's. D-O-U-L. In Alhambra."

The phone said, "For an additional charge of fifty cents, you'll be connected."

He lit a cigarette and inhaled deeply and blew smoke at the world. He took two clean breaths and punched the buttons.

"Let me talk to Juarez."

"Ain't no Juarez here."

"He's in the last booth with the Tall Man and that skinny girl the Tall Man hangs with who used to strip at the Top Down Club. Tell him it's Jimmy Luntz. Say I owe him money."

Juarez came on the line and said, "Jimmy," in an experimental tone of voice.

"Guess what? I smoked old Gambol in a rest stop on Highway 70," Luntz said.

He could feel Juarez swimming around in his own head, getting a grip on this information.

"Jimmy, you say this is Jimmy," Juarez repeated.

"Try spending five hours in a car going nowhere, and suddenly, oh, come to think of it, let's pull over here and get a piece of rebar from the trunk and give you a little compound fracture below the knee . . . You try it."

"Jimmy what. I mean, remind me of your last name," Juarez said.

"I told him let's go see Juarez," Luntz said, "and discuss the problem, you know? But he wouldn't allow it. As it is, I ended up defending myself."

"Sure, Jimmy. Could we talk about this? Could you maybe stop by?"

"Definitely not. Not in person. But I mean, I think you can show a little mercy, right?"

"This guy ain't making sense today," Juarez said, maybe to the Tall Man. "You are living in a happy dream," he told Luntz, "if you think there is any such thing as mercy."

Luntz hung up.

•

Jimmy Luntz drifted in the copper-tone Caddy alongside some kind of river, continuing north on 70, smoking his Camel and dropping the ashes on the floor. Gambol didn't let you smoke in his ride, but it wasn't his ride anymore, was it?

•

Anita took her vintage Camaro—her beat-up near-worthless 1973 Camaro—out under the willows by the Feather River and put on *Damn the Torpedoes* and dropped the seat all the way back and lay there with both doors open.

When the tape reached its end and would have reversed itself, the silence was such a blessing she hit the button and killed the power. Her hearing came up: the hiss of the river in this wide slow spot, and the breeze in the branches, the tick of willow leaves.

Only now did she begin to notice that the day was warm and fine. Or had been. The sunset shone down the river now, and the willows cast long shadows.

She grabbed her overcoat, a big blue thing with a velvet collar, got out of the Camaro, and tossed the coat down on the riverbank in the last patch of sun. A little dirt and leaves—who cares? She lay back and looked up at blue emptiness.

"TRY THE CAJUN CHICKEN," she shouted at the sky.

Hearing a vehicle, she sat upright. Across the river a copper-colored Cadillac with one of those cushy-looking vinyl roofs pulled to a stop at a campsite among a bunch of cottonwoods. A man in black dress pants and a white T-shirt got out holding what seemed very much like a large revolver.

He reversed the weapon in his grip, holding it by the barrel, and tossed it underhand into the river, his gaze following its arc out to the middle of the water and then across, beyond, to meet Anita's eyes watching him.

This guy didn't know much about follow-through. His throwing arm wavered in the air and collapsed at his side, and he wiped his fingers on his black slacks. A slouchy guy, a skinny guy. He wasn't wearing a Hawaiian shirt at the moment but undoubtedly possessed several.

He took in the fact of her without seeming particularly surprised, and then he got into his Cadillac and shut the door and started backing it up. But he wasn't leaving. He edged his ride into a shady spot and turned off the engine.

Anita considered this situation a minute before getting up and taking the keys from the Camaro's ignition and walking around to open its trunk. Inside she located two mayonnaise jars full of washers and screws, put one under each arm, and went around to the front of the car and took from the glove compartment a loaded stainless steel .357 Magnum.

She walked thirty feet across the bare spot where she'd parked and set the two jars on the dirt. She returned to the car, faced her targets, and took aim with a two-hand grip in what was often called the Weaver stance, the gun out front of her line of sight and both feet planted wide apart, elbows flexed and her shoulders slightly hunched, and fired twice.

Both jars exploded in a mist of glass and rusty nuts and bolts.

She lay down again on her coat, the gun resting on her belly, and let the day's last sunshine warm her on one side.

The sound of the Cadillac's engine came to her across the water, starting up and accelerating loudly as it took off—tires spinning, gravel rattling against the bark of trees—and then fading away.

•

Since sundown the temperature must have dropped twenty degrees. Luntz stopped in a movie theater parking lot in the town of Madrona and put on his shirt and white tux and sat listening to cool jazz on the Brougham's radio. The radio's clock display said 6:45.

When had he last eaten? He couldn't remember. He had no hunger. This, he told himself, is fear. So live with it.

He played with the radio on the AM band until he found a station that sounded likely—a young girl reading classified ads, mowers and pickups and appliances for sale by their owners. Then the local news. No gunplay reported. They mentioned the closing of a local supermarket.

Was Gambol a corpse? Were the cops after him, or not? How had everybody's day turned out?

He tried the FM band. Jamaican rhythms. Somebody sang

Nobody move
Nobody get hurt

—and he listened carefully to the rest of the song before turning off the radio.

The Rex Theater was showing *The Last Real Champ*,

according to the marquee. It was half over. Luntz bought a ticket anyway.

He sat leaning forward in the theater's second row with his forearms on the seat in front of him and his chin on his hands. In the film a guy followed a woman out of a bowling alley and caught her by the elbow, and she turned, and he said, "I'd throw everything away for a woman like you."

And she replied, "Really?" and you could tell they were headed for a happy ending.

In the final seconds of the final round the same guy rallied to destroy an opponent inexplicably forty pounds beyond his weight class. The defeated champion lay on the canvas, staring straight upward.

Early in his teens Luntz had fought Golden Gloves. Clumsy in the ring, he'd distinguished himself the wrong way—the only boy to get knocked out twice. He'd spent two years at it. His secret was that he'd never, before or since, felt so comfortable or so at home as when lying on his back and listening to the far-off music of the referee's ten-count.

After the film it was raining, a light, steady rain. Ruthless neon on the wet streets like busted candy. Eight p.m., dark enough to ditch the Cadillac. He drove it over to the town's tiny airport and parked and took the contents of his gym bag, the socks and underwear and toilet kit, and slipped them into Gambol's duffel and threw the gym bag into the darkness. He took off his black dress socks and put back on his shoes and wiped the car down with the socks, inside and outside, and left the keys under the floor mat and walked with Gambol's bag out of the parking lot and across a field of tall wet grass toward a couple of motels, the Ramada Inn and another one whose neon sign just said VACAN. The anonymous establishment, made of fake logs and cheap in its soul, looked like a place that didn't necessarily mess with credit cards.

He went over and booked a room. All wet, no car, no socks, paying cash.

•

The numbers on the radio read 10:10. Aces and zeroes. Luntz lay on his bed in the Guess What Motel on the Feather River Road with all the lights on listening to voices from a jerk-off movie in the next room.

Like the building's exterior, the walls of this small room looked like logs. He put his hand out and discovered he touched real wood. He hadn't known they still made things out of actual logs. He'd assumed all logs were fake.

He sat up and pointed the remote control at the television. Nothing happened. He slapped it against his palm and tried again unsuccessfully. He reached down and hefted Gambol's duffel bag from the floor beside him and sat up with his feet on the floor and his left hand resting on the bag for a good two minutes before pulling the zipper all the way from one end to the other.

The weapon inside, with its pistol grip and its gleaming chrome barrel about eighteen inches long, looked untouchable. He didn't touch it. He closed the zipper and stashed the bag under the bed and went out for some no-fake mountain air.

The rain had quit. He stood under a lot of stars, too many, more stars, in fact, than he'd ever seen. The chilly night air tasted clean and innocent. That lucky feeling came over him.

He walked across the parking lot to the lounge at the Ramada Inn and went directly to the pay phones by the restrooms in the back.

"Look," he said when he had O'Doul's on the phone, "I know he's sitting right there. Put him on. Tell him Luntz."

While he waited with his back to the lounge he heard the voices and smooth jazz. His hands were shaking and his throat was tight.

Juarez came on the line. "*Luntz*, is it now. Next thing you'll want to be *Mister* Luntz. Mister Luntz, *Esquire*."

"Yeah—you know how many holes a double-aught-buck shotgun shell is going to make in your face?"

"Where you calling from?"

"From the pay phone right outside where you're sitting."

"The fuck you are."

"I'm right out here on Fourth, señor, with Gambol's Winchester under my big old shirt. I'm looking right at you."

Juarez was talking to somebody else now—probably

sending the Tall Man outside to verify. "Where you from, Luntz—Luntzville? You ain't nothing but a little *puto*."

"Gambol said something similar. Then I blew him up."

"Guess what? He didn't die."

"Yeah, I didn't think so."

"Listen to me, Luntz. Do you remember this fucker Cal from Anaheim, they called him Cal Trans?"

"Yeah, sure, I heard all about that stuff."

"Gambol and I sat down and made a meal of his balls. Anaheim oysters. Very tasty."

"I heard all about it, yeah."

"What about Luntzville? They make pretty good oysters there?"

Luntz said, "Best oysters in the world, Juarez," and hung up.

•

She woke on the riverbank with rain falling on her face. She got up and closed herself inside the car. Burrowed into the big blue coat. Woke some time later stiff and cold, having slept deeply and freely.

She found the key and fired it up. Turned on the AM radio and caught a country station drifting over from Sparks, Nevada, while the engine warmed and the defroster blew the mist off the glass. Giant night of stars out there. She headed onto the highway.

The man from Sparks said it was 10:00 p.m. She'd

slept like the dead for nearly four hours. Eighteen months she'd spent fighting the judge and Hank, politicking the sheriff and the town council and harrying her lawyers and working the press, campaigning against the inevitable. Now it was over. Time for a long vacation. Not that she could afford even a short one.

At the lounge at the Ramada near the county airport she ordered a second tequila sunrise as the waitress delivered the first one. "And please, please," she said, "don't turn on the karaoke."

"I'll wait till eleven," the girl said.

"Just wait till I'm gone."

"Happy Hour starts at eleven."

"Then I'm working on a deadline."

Why do they call it happy, and why do they say it's an hour? Happy Hour lasts two miserable hours. Aah, she thought—who am I talking to? And how many seconds till some asshole offers to buy me a drink and make me a satisfied woman?

Approximately eighteen seconds. The same skinny guy from the river—the one who'd tossed the gun to the currents—coming back from the pay phone and toilets, now sporting a checkered vest and white tux over his T-shirt. He paused beside her booth. Exactly the cheap bastard for whom the two-dollar window was invented.

"Hey, there," he said.

"Very suave. You silver-tongued devil."

"Are you a resident of this motel, or just a patron?"

"I'm not anything," she said. "I'm having a drink."

He dropped something, a quarter, stooped to pick it up, dropped it, picked it up again, and stood looking around him as if the room had changed drastically in the two seconds he'd had his eyes off it. Not drunk. A little too vibrant for drunk.

He perched himself on the very outermost corner of the seat across from her, saying, "I don't usually just walk up and sit down with people."

"Help yourself. I was just leaving."

He peered at her, nearsighted or stupid, she couldn't tell which, and said, "What is your nationality?"

"What?"

"Are you a Spic?"

She stared. "Yeah. I am. Are you an asshole?"

"Mostly," he said.

"What's your name?"

He said, "Uh."

"Uh? What is Uh? Lithuanian or something?"

"You're witty," he said. "My name's Frank. Franklin."

"Frankie Franklin," she said, "I have a lot on my mind right now, and I'd like to be alone."

"No problemo," he said, and kind of oozed out of the booth and dematerialized.

The barmaid brought her a second tequila sunrise while she ordered a third. "Hey, miss," Anita said, "when do we get this karaoke rolling?"

Luntz watched it all unwind. The woman was the hit of the evening, at least in her own opinion. She sat on a stool she'd dragged from the bar and placed exactly next to the karaoke contraption, nobody daring to interfere with this spectacle—singing half a song and talking through the rest of it and selecting another through two hours of encores, but nobody called for them.

She wore a blue coat over the same gray skirt and white blouse he'd seen her in that afternoon by the river. A good-looking woman. With or without makeup, in any style of clothes, drunk or sober. "Thank you very much, I love this town!" she said many, many times.

She stopped reading the lyrics on the screen and made up her own instead, and then stopped singing the melodies and made those up too, closing her eyes and riffing about a guy named Hank who walked with the devil.

"That woman needs a pill," the waitress said.

Luntz disagreed. "Man," he said, "she breaks your heart."

Once in a while Luntz went out to smoke a cigarette under the stars. The rest of the time he stood by the cash-out playing the scratch-off instant lottery, rubbing one by one at the numbers in a stack an inch thick, tossing the losers on the counter till he had quite a pile. He spent eighty bucks and made back sixty-five.

By 1:00 a.m. she'd cleared the place out and was just drinking and muttering into the microphone while the waitress chatted with the barmaid.

"I believe," the woman said into her microphone, with plenty of reverb, "that's Frankie Franklin over there. He's piling up them lotto tix."

He raised a hand high and gave her a thumbs-up.

"What is Frankie about to do with them lotto tix? Make himself a little bonfire?"

She punched buttons on the machine and after thirty seconds of music jumped onto the chorus—"Come on baby light my fi-yer! Come on baby light my fi-yer!" She stopped singing and her gaze drifted down and sideways, and she smiled at nothing.

Luntz walked over. "Can I ask a favor? I need a ride."

"You do?"

"I do. I really do."

"Where's Frankie's Cadillac?"

"Oh. The Caddy. Yeah."

"I saw you by the river, Frankie. Remember?"

"I wouldn't forget seeing you."

"Caddy end up in the river too?"

"It was a loaner. So how about a ride to my motel?"

"Call a cab."

"I was thinking you'd be quicker."

"Which motel?"

"The Log Inn over there."

"Across the parking lot? Very funny."

"I'm witty, too, just like you."

"The Log Inn. Doesn't the wood stink when it's wet?"

"So how about a ride?"

"I don't drive a cab. Hey, Frankie. Let me buy a round. What are you drinking?"

"This is a Diet Coke."

"Don't you drink?"

He paused for a good little while before he answered.

"I gamble," he said.

"And what about for a living? If it's not too forward of me. What do you do?"

"I gamble. I gamble."

"What's the point of gambling?"

"I didn't realize there had to be a point."

"This is starting to sound like one of those messed-up conversations," she said.

"You could get me a can of beer, but I probably wouldn't finish it. My stomach burns easy. I can't even drink coffee."

She raised her mike to her lovely mouth and looked over at the waitress and said, "I better have some coffee myself. Black, please." Up close, in somber light, he couldn't say if she was supposed to be a Mexican or Hawaiian or some semi-Filipino mutt.

"Where are you from originally?"

"The rez."

"What?"

"The reservation."

"What?"

"Yeah."

The waitress brought her a Styrofoam cup and she dribbled half the coffee down her blouse and was completely unapologetic about it. "I don't need coffee anyway. I can't sleep anyway lately."

"You too? Me neither."

"I didn't sleep for two days, and then I had a nap."

"Two days? Why?"

"Because I didn't have a bed, Frankie. What about you? Why can't you sleep?"

"Too many plans on my mind. It's been one heck of a day."

She peered at him. "You too?"

"So, anyway," Luntz said.

She stood up, said, "Thank you very much! I love this town!" and walked out the door into the night.

Luntz went after her because he just couldn't stand it.

She stood out front digging in her purse with one hand, nearly choking herself with the strap.

"I'd throw everything away for a woman like you."

"Jesus Christ," she said, and walked with considerable difficulty the twenty feet to her little hotrod.

He stood and watched while she searched for the driver's seat with her beautiful ass. She saw him watching and gave him the finger and slammed the door.

Luntz headed in the other direction, toward the end of the building and the parking lot across which waited the

Log Inn. After thirty seconds listening to his own steps on the pavement he heard her tires screech, and next the sound of her engine rising and falling and rising again, and then coming up behind him.

Stopping for him, she nearly ran him down. While he got in the car the dome light illuminated her dimly, staring straight ahead, stupid-drunk. "I can do anything I want," she said.

•

The first two things she did on entering were to throw her purse on the bed and then go to the nightstand and pick up his checkered bow tie. She examined it and turned to him, holding it to her throat.

Luntz said, "Boy, I'd like to see you wearing just that and nothing else."

She kicked her high heels off and said, "May I have a glass of water, please?"

He filled the plastic cup in the john and brought it to her and she drained it in under five seconds, gasping between swallows, and headed for the john herself, saying, "Refill." She didn't stagger, but she walked very carefully.

Luntz picked up his bow tie and stood staring at it.

On his bed, the woman's purse started chirping. Luntz said, "Should I get your phone?"

She came out through the bathroom door, grabbed her cell phone from a side pocket in her purse, and went back into the bathroom and tossed the phone in the toilet. She hiked her skirt and yanked her pantyhose to her knees and sat down, all in one motion, and started peeing kind of musically.

Luntz said, "Hold my calls."

He stood in the bathroom doorway watching, and as she reached back for the handle, failing to locate it, he said, "Welcome to my humble origins."

"It *does* stink when it's wet."

She came out with another cup of water and drank it down and exhaled loudly. She kissed him wetly on the lips, tasting of booze and just a bit like something else even worse, puke, maybe, but he didn't care. She drew back and said, "You think I'm just too hammered to know better."

"Yeah, I do, and I thank God."

"Nope. I know where I am. I know where up is."

She stepped away from him and pointed at the ceiling. "Good."

"It's just, it's just, hey—it's feeling good right now to be around somebody who's not full of shit up to his eyeballs."

"Are you kidding? I'm the most fulla shit guy I know."

"Well," she assured him, "you're not the most fulla shit guy *I* know." She grabbed the hem of her coffee-stained white blouse and wrestled it up over her head, but could only raise it so far, and she appeared to be lost in it, wavering side to side in her crimson bra. "Not even close," she said. Fell backward onto the bed, her arms and head tangled in her blouse, one tit coming out of its red cup and the gray skirt hiked up nearly to her crotch and her feet dangling off the mattress.

Luntz grabbed her ankles and swung her legs around so she lay out straight. He hooked his fingers into the elastic waistline and pulled her skirt and pantyhose down both together. Her body seemed slack. She might have passed out. "Tough break," he said. But he only meant for her.

He took off his tux, his checkered vest, the T-shirt, the pants.

She was conscious after all. She plucked at the blouse wrapped around her head and got it down below the level of her eyes and looked at him, speaking through its folds, stark naked below her waist. "So—are you a waiter?"

"What?"

"Is that what the tux is about?"

"No. I'm in a barbershop chorus."

"Like a quartet."

"No. Bigger, between eighteen and thirty guys, depending on who shows up. I'm in a quartet sometimes too. But the quartet's not that good. We don't practice."

"But not your chorus. Your chorus is good, huh?"

"No. We're not that good either."

"Frankie Franklin, are you a loser?"

"Not when I'm lucky."

"When was a guy like you ever lucky?"

He pulled her blouse over her head and a couple of buttons popped loose and flew at his face. "Shit, honey," he said, "have you looked at yourself in the mirror lately? I'm lucky now."

•

Gambol was able to see, but nothing he saw made sense. Yet it wasn't quite like dreaming. He closed his eyes.

A woman's voice spoke some words, then the same words once more, and again the same words.

He said, "Fuck off."

•

He seemed to have fallen from a narrow bed and now found himself jammed in a space even narrower. He sighed.

A woman said, "Jesus. Well—at least you're moving. Can you sit up?"

He said, "Leave me alone."

"At least get back up here and lie straight."

He said, "No. Fuck off."

He realized he was staring at the roof of a car's interior. Every time he breathed, he heard the slight creaking of plastic.

Later he deduced he must be lying on a plastic sheet inside a car.

The woman was talking again. "Yeah. You're a major mess today. Can you sit up?"

"Fuck off."

"If you can move, I want you inside."

"Inside."

"Sit up. Sit up. One stage at a time."

•

He was sitting on a couch, his injured leg stretched out on an ottoman. He was looking at a television in a small living room with a woman who said, "Wow, do you ever feel like you're just in the future? I mean, like science fiction?"

"Shut up. Who are you?"

"I told you who I am."

"The fuck you did."

"Then who have I been talking to for the last half hour?"

"I didn't hear us talking."

"How's the pain?"

The pain, though it belonged to his right leg, radiated in astounding waves out to his toes and up to his jaw. "Real bad."

She put a bowl beside him on the couch. "I want you to suck on some ice. Just to keep your throat lubricated."

Some of the pain made it all the way to his right eyeball and also the tip of his nose.

"Are you there?"

"I'm somewhere."

"It hurts," she said. "I know. It hurts."

"You got any dope?"

"Not yet. It's coming."

"Fuck."

"Hang in there."

"Fuck. Jesus Christ."

"Don't choke on that ice."

"Fuck. Fuck."

Fighting the pain only made it worse. Gambol paid attention to the pain, to its shape, its location, and its travels, and tried to stay relaxed.

•

A doorbell rang. Voices spoke in another world, where people had thoughts worth voicing. Laughter. Silence.

She came to him with a hypo and said, "The cavalry has arrived." By this time the pain had conquered every physical part of him and had begun to involve his soul. Then the sensations flattened out and got hard to locate, and as long as he didn't try moving, things were pretty jolly.

•

"You ready for some water?"

"Yeah."

She brought him a glass with a straw. He could hardly swallow, but it was sweet. "Drink as much as you can. Watch your IV, hon. Don't move that hand around. Other hand."

He hadn't noticed the drip in his left wrist. "I feel paralyzed."

"I couldn't give you any blood."

"Yeah. A person can't live on horse blood, right?"

"What?"

"You're a vet, right?"

She laughed and said something he couldn't hear.

•

She woke him and fed him some pills and held the glass while he sucked at the straw until the glass was empty. The light around them seemed like morning light. But it might have been evening. "You got any coffee?"

"Coffee won't help right now."

"Just give me a cup of coffee."

The smell was wonderful, but it tasted wrong coming through a straw. "Just let me drink it."

"Sure."

His hand felt like a senseless mitten. She helped him hook his finger through the cup's handle.

"Give me the fucking thing."

"I just gave it to you. Relax."

She turned on the television. He sipped his coffee and stared at the colorful screen.

After a while he said, "I need a car. And I need a gun."

PART TWO

PART TWO

PART TWO

JIMMY LUNTZ woke at the Log Inn Motel and spent twenty minutes sitting upright in his bed, smoking a Camel and staring at the woman asleep beside him. Just watching her breathe. Very gently he lifted the covers. She was dark-skinned all the way down. "Oh, that's right," he said, "you're an Indian."

The woman didn't stir.

He carried his shaving kit into the bathroom. Before he emptied his bladder he fished the woman's cell phone out of the toilet and set it on top of the tank. Anita. She hadn't told him her last name.

He took his time shaving, grooming, getting good. He couldn't remember the last time he'd awakened beside an unfamiliar woman. As for one this good-looking—never.

He came out naked and found her wide awake, sitting on the bed's edge. Also naked. Holding a revolver in one hand.

With the other hand she held up a credit card. "What's this?"

"Wow," he said, "you tell me."

"What is it?"

"It looks like American Express," he said. "Wow."

"You said your name was Franklin."

"Well, it's not."

"It's Ernest Gambol."

"It's not that either."

She spun the credit card from her fingers, and it sailed across the room. "Then what *is* your name, if you don't mind my asking, since we recently fucked, and all."

"Jimmy Luntz."

"Who's Ernest Gambol?"

"Gambol is a great big asshole."

"As big an asshole as you?"

"Bigger. Just my opinion."

"In my opinion, the asshole is the one who steals the wallet."

"The thing about a gun," Luntz said, "is it can just go off."

"I'm not pointing it at you."

"I'm talking about this other gun."

"What other gun?"

"The one I shot Gambol with."

She closed her knees together and took hold of the blanket and pulled it over her crotch. "*Now* it's pointing at you."

"You don't have to tell me. That's all I can look at, is that gun."

"That's what I thought yesterday. I saw you at the Feather River, remember? I thought, Hey, that guy has a gun. Then—sploosh. No more gun."

"I saw you too."

She aimed her weapon at him a long time without speaking. She stood up. Luntz stepped backward until his shoulders collided with the wall.

With her purse in one hand and her gun in the other she headed for the can and shut the door behind her. The lock clicked. Luntz heard the shower start. He let the air out of his lungs.

He lit up and burned through half a Camel, inhaling smoke with every breath.

With the cigarette clamped in his lips he went on his hands and knees and pulled Gambol's white duffel bag from under the bed and opened it. He found his last clean set of socks and underwear. He didn't touch Gambol's shotgun.

He got on his socks and shorts and opened his door and tossed the last burning inch of his cigarette into the parking lot and observed a county squad car pulling up to the motel's office. A green Caprice, mid-nineties.

Luntz sat on the bed and wrapped himself in his own arms and closed his eyes and sat there shaking his head.

As soon as the knocking came he started for the door, but three feet short of it he stopped. He cleared his throat and said, "Who is it?"

"Sheriff's deputy."

"Two seconds."

Luntz put his hand on the doorknob and bowed his head and waited for a thought that didn't arrive. Four more knocks. He opened the door and said, "Good morning!" to a young guy in uniform.

"Good morning. Mr. Franklin, right? How are you?"

"Me?" Luntz said. "Better and better."

"That's good. Do you know anything about a Cadillac parked over there at the airstrip?"

"No. A Cadillac?"

"There's a Cadillac Brougham parked over there, and Mr. Nabilah tells me you checked in without a car."

"Me? Yeah. No. I mean, that's right. Who's Mr. Nabilah?"

"The manager. He thought it might be your Caddy over there."

"Right. Oh. Yeah."

"And it looks like blood on the left rear tire, lotta blood. Did you maybe hit a dog?"

"No. It's not my car. I don't have a car."

"There's a hole in the left rear quarter panel. Looks like a bullet hole."

"For goodness' sake," Luntz said.

"Can I see some ID?"

"ID? Sure. Gee—where's my pants?"

At that moment Anita came out of the bathroom wrapped in a towel, her black hair slicked back, and flashed a smile that would have blown the doors off Jesus Christ. "Deputy Rabbit!"

"That's me," the deputy said, and then—"Oh. Mrs. . . ."

"Right, it's still Mrs. Desilvera," she said. "For six more months."

"Oh, right," the deputy said, "that's your Camaro out there. I mean, it looked like it. I mean—yeah. That's your car." He turned to look at her car, which was parked sideways across three spaces behind him.

"All mine. Is there a problem?"

"No problem. I was just checking about this Caddy out there at the airstrip. If nobody claims it, I'll have to get it towed."

"Tow it to the moon," Luntz said. "It ain't my car."

"He's with me," Anita said.

"Okay, that clears things up a little. Thanks."

"Glad to help," Anita said. "Can I get dressed?"

"That's fine," the deputy said.

"Are you going to watch?"

"Oh!" he said, and laughed. "All righty. Have a nice day, folks."

Luntz said, "You too," and shut the door in his face and sat down on the bed.

Anita dropped her towel and stepped into her skirt. Luntz stared at her breasts.

She got her bra fastened. "That was Deputy Rabbit."

"Maybe his first name is Jack, huh?"

"Deputy Rabbit conducted my firearms training class."

"You actually have a carry permit or something?"

"I did. But it's revoked." She found her blouse on the floor. "Deputy Rabbit was talking about your Caddy."

"It's not my Caddy."

"It was your Caddy when I saw you throw that gun in the Feather River."

"I just borrowed it."

"The gun? Or the car?"

"Both."

"What did you say your name was?"

"Jimmy."

"Can I borrow the Cadillac, Jimmy?"

"What's wrong with that Camaro of yours?"

"Too many people know it."

"Like Deputy Rabbit, you mean."

"Can I have the keys?"

"The door's unlocked," he said. "I put the keys under the floor mat. But I wouldn't advise driving around in that thing."

"Is it stolen?"

"Not legally, I guess. Gambol doesn't deal with the police."

"Gambol? I thought you shot him."

"He didn't die."

"Is he running around looking for it?"

"Probably not. Not yet. If he is, he's running around on one leg."

Luntz stared while she sat on the bed and stuck her toes into the legs of her pantyhose and stood up straight and hiked her skirt and wiggled her underwear all the way on. She dropped the hem and smoothed her skirt. One at a time she kicked her black pumps into position on the floor and worked her feet into them. She got her coat on and opened the door.

"Wait a minute," Luntz said, "I want to talk to you. I mean, about last night."

"What was your name again?"

"Jimmy Luntz. I had a good time last night."

"It was kind of a fluke, Jimmy."

"I get that. Yeah. But maybe we could have coffee or something."

Leaving the front door ajar, she went into the john and came back and handed him her cell phone. "Hang on to this phone. If it still works, maybe I'll call you."

She gave him a little salute and walked out, and he sat there holding her phone in his hand for ten minutes.

Then he set the cell phone aside, clapped his hands together twice, and stood up. He got dressed and got his gear together. He had no jacket other than his white tuxedo. He put it on and pocketed the cell phone. He picked up Gambol's duffel by the handle and looked around for anything he might have forgotten. A knock came at the door.

He opened it quickly. It wasn't Anita.

Two very clean-cut men stood side by side in the

doorway, one of them holding up a badge. "We're with the Federal Bureau of Investigation."

Luntz said, "Wow."

The man put his badge away and told Luntz both their names, but Luntz didn't hear.

"Wow," he said. "For a second I thought you were Jehovah Witness people."

"Can I ask your name, sir?"

"Franklin. But listen—I'm about to hop on a bus. I'm late."

"Where's Mrs. Desilvera, Mr. Franklin?"

"Mrs. who?"

"The lady staying here with you."

"Oh. I didn't get her last name. Just her first."

"Are you two pretty good friends?"

"They're on a first-name basis," the other one said.

"I just met her last night."

"Yes. We're aware of that."

The other one said, "What's in your bag? Two million dollars?"

"What?"

"Didn't she tell you she's sitting on a pile of other people's money?"

"We barely got introduced."

"We understand that," the nicer one said. "Did she say where she was going?"

"No, sir. Destination unknown."

"Let me tell you what this is about, Mr. Franklin. In

just a few days your friend will plead guilty to embezzling two-point-three million dollars." He waited for a reaction and seemed satisfied with Luntz's speechlessness.

"You didn't know about it?" the other one said.

"No, sir. No. Embezzlement—that's a federal thing, huh?"

"She'll plead guilty to state charges. But until the money goes back where it belongs, we're very interested in her. Federal charges aren't out of the question. Can you show us some identification?"

Luntz dug out his driver's license and handed it over.

"I thought you said your name was Franklin."

"Yeah—but that's when I didn't know who you were."

"I told you who we were."

"Oh," Luntz said, "that's correct. I guess I got confused. I thought you guys were Jehovah's Witnesses."

"Really?"

"Look, I have to catch a bus south in fifteen minutes. I mean, now it's ten minutes."

"When will you be seeing Mrs. Desilvera again?"

"Never. I got the impression it was, you know—a fluke."

"A fluke?"

"That's the description I'm giving it."

"What's in the bag? That's not her bag, is it?"

"It's mine. It's my luggage, is all."

"I bet you wish it was her luggage."

"So she still has the money, huh?"

"Was she carrying anything, Mr. Luntz?"

"You mean like a satchel with a big old dollar sign on it?"

Neither of them laughed.

"Just a purse," Luntz said. "About yay big."

"You mind if we look around the room?"

"Help yourself. I'm all checked out. And I'm really late, so—yeah."

The nicer one raised an index finger. "Call coming in." He took a few paces backward, and the other one joined him and stood with his back to Luntz, the first one with his phone to his cheek, talking. It seemed the other might be talking too. Fake phone call. Luntz lit a cigarette while they reached an agreement.

"Okay if I get moving?"

"That'll be fine. We'll make a note of your name, Mr. Luntz."

"Okay. I sure hope I make that bus."

They stepped aside for him, and the nicer one said, "Good luck."

"I was born lucky."

Luntz set out at a good pace without a backward glance. He had no idea where he was going.

In his pocket, the cell phone started ringing.

•

Gambol closed his eyes. He felt his head nodding forward and rode a Ferris wheel down into violent cartoons.

He shivered, but he didn't feel cold. When he shivered the pain filled his right leg.

"I want another shot."

"Not for two more hours," the woman said. "This isn't an opium den."

He opened his eyes. He wore a frilly blue nylon robe. Probably the woman's.

"Where's my clothes?"

"How many times are you going to ask me that?"

"Fuck you."

"Your stuff went out with the rest of the bloody trash."

Gambol's head drooped, and he looked down into Jimmy Luntz's face.

•

The landscape had that blond, Central Valley look. Some pine trees. Oaks. Orchards. Farmland. Sunny and still. They drove south past Oroville, looking for a shopping mall. The speed signs said 65. Luntz stayed legal. He kept his window cracked to suck his cigarette smoke away from Anita's face.

Luntz said, "Dude who worked in a casino in Vegas told me about this hippie. This hippie comes in out of the desert night, creeps into the casino all scraggly in his huarache sandals and tie-dye shirt and Hindu balloon pants, and he goes to the roulette table and reaches into this little pouch tied to his belt and comes up with one U.S. quarter. Lays the quarter on black. Little ball comes down on twenty-two black. He lets it ride, doubles again, switches to red, doubles his dollar, takes his two dollars to the blackjack and wins ten in a row, doubling every time. Ten in a row. True story. Two thousand and forty-eight dollars. He pulls his chips and heads for the craps and starts betting with the shooter, double whatever the shooter bets. Inside of two hours the house is clocking his action and he's comped with free meals and he's drunk on free booze, and he's still at the craps, with a crowd around him, betting a couple hundred a throw. By three a.m. he's stacked up over six grand off an initial investment of twenty-five cents. And suddenly, in four or five big bets, all gone—he busts out. Stands there thinking a minute . . . folks around him watching . . . He stands there . . . Everybody's shouting, "One more quarter! One more quarter!" Old hippie shakes his head. Staggers back out into the desert after one hell of a night in a Vegas casino. A night they're still talking about. Total cost was twenty-five cents. A night he'll never forget."

"For a person who doesn't drink coffee," Anita said, "you sure run your mouth."

"It keeps me from thinking about things."

"Like what?"

"Like who you are and what the fuck you want."

•

Cigarette smoke in his nostrils woke Gambol, and he coughed, and the woman said, "Sorry," waving it away.

"Lots of folks are quitting these days."

"What century are you in, guy? I'm the last smoker on earth."

"How long have I been here?"

"You don't remember yesterday?"

"When was yesterday?"

"You were walking and talking."

"Walking?"

"And swearing. In a real creative style. I poked my head into that culvert, and you hopped right up and walked right to my car. Then," she said, "I couldn't get you out of the car. I had to do the whole thing in the back seat. Debrided the wound and all the rest. The back seat of a Chevy Lumina is not the place for that."

Gambol closed his eyes. "I feel like I weigh ten tons."

"You lost a lot of blood. A lot. I scored one liter of plasma. Nothing else but glucose and water."

"Feels like he shot me through the bone."

"He missed the bone. Or you'd be in the ER right now getting your leg saved and probably talking to a detective."

"I don't talk to detectives."

"And he missed the big artery, or you'd be dead."

•

At the Time Out Lounge in the Oroville Mall they sat in the rearmost booth, and Jimmy who called himself Franklin only stared at her, never sipping once from his Coke. She took a long swallow of vodka-and-Seven and said, "Oh, well . . . was I on TV again?"

"How did you steal two-point-three million bucks?"

"Didn't the TV tell you? You run a bond election for a new high school, you float the loan, turn on the computers, transfer it here and there—zip, all yours."

"That's greedy."

"Then the money gets missed right away, and the list of suspects is extremely short. Then somebody gets arrested."

"Well," he said.

"Well, what?"

"I guess you were greedy enough to take it, but not mean enough to frame an asshole. Excuse my language," he added, "but where I come from that's what they call the guy who gets sacrificed—the asshole."

She laughed without feeling amused. "There was definitely an asshole," she said.

"If you've got it stashed, you're doing it right, wandering around acting broke. That's doing it right. But if you've got it, why don't you just disappear?"

"For one thing, I'm due in court to enter a plea and take a deal. Probation and lifelong restitution. If I miss that date, the judge'll void the deal and max me out. That's six years at least."

"Kind of a long time to wait to spend your two million."

"Have you lost count already? Two-point-three."

"What's a point or three among friends?"

"I haven't got any friends. And I'm flat broke."

"Not according to the Federal Bureau of Jehovah's Witnesses."

"I haven't got the money. I just know who has it and how to get it."

No more flip commentary from Mr. Jimmy.

"Doesn't that interest you?"

"You're interesting every way there is."

•

This Jimmy was your basic bus-station javelina, but a nice enough guy. He insisted on handing her two Ben Franklin hundreds before they left the lounge. "You're with me now."

"That's not established."

"By 'now' I just mean now—right this second. That gets you at least a couple hundred."

He led her into JCPenney's, where he stacked generic-looking items on one of his arms and went into the dressing room wearing his shiny black pants and white tuxedo and came out in khaki chinos and a flannel Pendleton.

"Where's your fancy threads?"

"On the floor in there. I shed those babies like a sunburn."

"You're fast."

"These days, life is fast."

She picked out a JCPenney pantsuit, a JCPenney blouse, a JCPenney skirt, and the best underwear they had, which wasn't much. While Jimmy stood around waiting for her she sat in the dressing room momentarily naked with these latest humiliations at her feet and rage in her heart. JCPenney.

She changed into the pantsuit, gray pinstripe, and made sure she had her shoulders back and her smile on before she swept aside the curtain. "Does it fit?"

He stared, and then he went for his Camels and put one between his lips, realized where he was, dropped the cigarette into his shopping bag. "It fits."

"You're sweet," she said, and she sort of meant it. But not as a compliment. "You're homeless, right?"

"I have a home. I'm just not going back there, is all."

"So right in that shopping bag is everything you own."

"Everything I need."

"And your white canvas bag—what's in that one?"

"Everything else I need."

"I know what's in it. A sawed-off shotgun."

He seemed completely unsurprised. "It's not a sawed-off. It's a pistol-grip. And it isn't mine."

"I peeked in the bag while you were in the shower."

"You zipped it up real nice," he said. "Good for you."

•

Jimmy Luntz drove the Caddy north. He watched the dial and kept under the limit. Again they passed through the blond country. Some vineyards here and there, lots of vineyards. Either vineyards, or orchards with very small trees. He asked her if those were vineyards.

"What do you care? Are you a wino?" Anita drank from an extra-large Sprite in a go-cup, doctoring it with vodka.

Orchards. A roadside stand selling Asian pears spelled ASIAIN PEARS. Then higher country, the road winding. They lost the jazz station. He found another, just geezer rock. Tight curves, tall pines, and geezer rock. "Is that the Feather River?"

By way of answer, she took a swig and coughed.

"Hell of a lot of trees," he said.

"That's why they call it the forest. I hope we're not going camping."

"We are if I can't find this place before dark."

"Look, Jimmy—who is this guy?"

"I knew him in Alhambra."

"Is that a prison?"

"It's a city a few hundred miles from here. In your state. California."

She pushed the button and her window came down and the wind thudded in the car as she pitched her empty and listened for the small musical sound of the bottle shattering behind them.

"You're nice," he said, "when you're sober."

"Have you ever seen me sober?"

"I think I did for about a minute."

She lay her head back on the headrest and closed her eyes.

Luntz turned down the radio and kept his eyes going left and right, looking for a building, a sign, anything.

After a while she opened her eyes. "What's the plan?"

"So far the plan is I can't go back and I can't stay here. That's the plan so far."

"You know what I mean. What's the plan?"

Luntz stalled for twenty seconds, starting a cigarette. He set his lighter between them on the console. "I think if you're looking for a gunslinger, you better keep looking."

"You said you shot Gambol."

"Only in the leg. I should've put two more in his head, just in proper observance of the rules. Instead I took pity. You don't want a guy with pity in his heart."

"I'd like to know what the plan is."

"I didn't say yes yet. Let's sit down with a paper and pen and map out the pros and cons."

"Great."

"Don't say great yet. Say great when I say yes."

"I just hope I chose the right guy." When Luntz said nothing, she added, "Don't be insulted."

"I'm not insulted. I just think it's bullshit for you to act like you had a choice."

•

The woman was what they called a hefty blonde, in jeans and a sweatshirt and big pink fuzzy slippers. She smoked cigarettes and watched crime shows and fake judges on TV while Gambol nodded out and watched cartoons in his head. She laughed a lot at the shows, and when she laughed it woke him up, and he watched her.

"Where's the vet?"

"Vet?"

"Juarez said he knew a vet could fix me."

"A vet, huh? I guess that's me."

"What kind of animals? Large? Like cattle? Or small like pets?"

She laughed, took a drink from her glass—some kind of booze—and set it down and lit a cigarette. "I'm a *veteran*. I was an army nurse for twenty-one years, three months, and six days. Dealt with lots of combat trauma." She exhaled straight upward to avoid blowing smoke in his face. "I'm a veteran. Not a veterinarian."

"What's your name, lady?"

"Mary. What's yours?"

"Fuck you."

"That's what I thought."

He nodded off and shot Luntz four times in the crotch, waited while he suffered, and then left him with two in the head.

•

In the last light they parked the Caddy and got out. Behind the building the ground sloped toward a tiny shantytown by the river, half a dozen trailers, pickup trucks, a couple motorcycles. She asked him if this was some sort of gang hideout, and he said it was the Feather River Tavern, that's all.

They entered a large café with a torn-up floor and secondhand tables and a view of spectacular cottonwoods dropping their seed tufts on the river in the dusk, and the trailers.

Jimmy glanced at the man behind the counter and said, "Wow," and sat down at a table with his back to the counter. "Sit there," he told Anita.

She sat across from him. "Is that him?"

"He's not the one I want." Jimmy sat touching his fingertips together. "He looking?"

"No."

Jimmy glanced over his shoulder at the man once more, quickly, and said, "Okay, I'll hit the head. Ask him about selling a Harley. Like we've got a bike to sell. Don't mention any names."

"He's coming over."

Jimmy stood. "Get me a Coke, okay?" He touched her arm with two fingers as he walked past her.

The other man approached. He was slumped and bony, and the knees of his jeans brushed together as he walked. "Got a special today. Trout." He wore a red headband around a shaggy gray mullet.

"Maybe just a couple Cokes, please."

Behind the counter he opened two cans and poured them into glasses with ice, all the while looking at her with something other than the hunger of a man. Something more like envy. After she'd reached puberty, her mother had looked at her like that.

He brought her the Cokes and set them down, each with a cocktail napkin. His fingers were long, the fingernails too. On his left ring finger he wore a large turquoise.

Anita said, "I have a Harley I might like to sell. Do you know anybody who could point me in the right direction?"

"John's out back. He'd be the one."

She sipped her Coke and wished for vodka. Jimmy came back from the can, hiding his face by wiping his nose with a paper towel, and sat down across from Anita again. "What did he say?"

"He said John's out back."

"That's the one I want."

He tossed down a five, and they left their Cokes and cocktail napkins and went out the front way and around the side of the building. Jimmy headed down the slope. She removed her high heels and followed, taking each step toes-first and dangling the pumps from the fingers of either hand.

Beside a teardrop aluminum trailer, a bearded biker in denim overalls sat on a flat-back chair, messing with an old guitar, the guitar flat on his lap and his head bent low. He didn't raise his face from this operation but said, "Getting too dark to see this shit."

Jimmy said, "Can you actually play that thing, Jay? I didn't know that."

"Got to get the strings in it first."

Jimmy said nothing more. The man raised his head. He placed his hands flat on his guitar. "I think what I want to say right here is, 'What is the meaning of this?'"

Jimmy took a white handkerchief from his back pocket, spread it on the trailer's step, seated himself, and said, "First of all."

The biker looked Anita over and then turned facing Jimmy and said nothing.

Jimmy said, "I'm not out to snitch on anybody, that's the first thing. All secrets remain completely secret."

"So far so good."

"This is Anita. This is my friend John Capra. We call him Jay."

The man rose halfway and said to Anita, "You want to sit down?" She shook her head. He sat back down and held the guitar gently in his lap. "It's a strange world."

"Did you notice Santa Claus stopping by here one time last spring? That guy we call Santa Claus?"

"With the white beard."

"Works in a mall every Christmas."

"I saw him," Capra said. "I didn't think he saw me."

"Yeah. He did."

"Say hi to him next time."

"No," Luntz said, "no next time for me."

Capra kept quiet.

Jimmy placed his elbows on his knees and leaned

forward. "Who's that dude in there, Capra? In the café. That's Sally Fuck."

"Just possibly. If so, his name would be Sol Fuchs. He's against being called Fuck. But the thing is—last names, man." Capra plucked one of the strings and turned a key on the instrument's neck and tightened it to a whine. "This is a pretty fucked-up situation. We're incognito here, you know?"

"All of us. All of us."

Anita held out her hand and said, "Anita Desilvera. And this is my friend Jimmy Luntz."

Capra took her hand gently and said, "Okay. Now all our dicks are hanging out."

"Pleased and charmed."

Capra laughed. He stopped laughing. "Fucking Santa Claus. Who else knows?"

"Whoever he told. Nobody believed him."

"You did."

"Not really. But I'm in a wild mood, so I'm taking any long shot, anything looks like action."

"What do you need, Jimmy?"

"Remember that time I let you stay with me and Shelly?"

"I owe you, Jimmy. That's a fact."

"We need to hunker down a minute. Get some options figured out."

Capra tangled his fingers in his beard and yanked at it. "How many days? I hope it's days, man, and not weeks."

"I don't know."

"Don't matter none. I owe you. But it's Sol's place, not mine. All I can do is talk to Sol."

Anita said, "Till next Wednesday."

"What's today?"

"I don't know."

"Saturday," Jimmy said.

"Wednesday's probably acceptable." Capra stood and set his guitar down on the seat of his chair and started up the hill. By now it was dark.

At the bottom of the staircase up the building's side Jimmy waited while she brushed the soles of her feet and put her shoes on, and then they climbed behind Capra up to the small landing. Capra worked a key and let them in and flipped a wall switch. A bed, a stove, a fridge. Wooden floor with the finish scratched off. For a curtain, a bedsheet. "You can eat in the restaurant for the usual price, or you can make a list and I'll bring you shit from the store in a box. It's up to you. I'll get Sol to go along as far as Wednesday."

From beneath them, Anita felt the gigantic quiet of the empty establishment downstairs. "Is the restaurant closed?"

"Open for business. But most of the folks who come here are down in Bolinas for the biker convention." Capra looked her up and down and seemed to examine her face carefully. "So what happens Wednesday?"

"Wednesday I go to court."

"Yeah. I know you."

"Nobody knows me."

"You're slightly infamous."

"All lies," Anita said.

"So!" Jimmy said. "John Capra didn't die."

"Nope. My old lady wanted alimony. That's unacceptable. I cut her some slack. I walked."

"Like a real gentleman," Anita said.

"Yeah, it was, lady. I know twenty dudes would've taken her out to the Mojave and buried her alive for that shit."

"I didn't mean it," Anita said.

Capra put his hand on the doorknob and stared at her, but he was speaking to Jimmy. "This one got the beauty that goes down to the bone. High heels or barefoot, don't matter."

"She can sing too."

"I can't tell if she's powered by a lot of soul or a lot of psycho electricity."

Anita said, "Do you always talk about people like they're invisible?"

"Usually just women."

It was one of those hippie-student pads smelling like cat shit, incense, a little dirty laundry, dirty dishes. She said, "Does somebody, you know—clean?" just to be a bitch.

"I said I owe him. I didn't say I was his slave." Capra shut the door softly behind him, and the windowpanes rattled as he went down the stairs.

Jimmy lit a cigarette and said, "Honey? I'm home!"

Anita said, "Is this a smoking room?"

"Yeah. I smoke."

"Well, fine. Smoke."

He blew smoke and opened what looked like a closet door. "Even a bathroom. No tub."

Anita sat on the bed. "Jeez, the mattress is like quicksand, help!"

"Don't get lost. I'll be back." He went out the door, and she listened to the panes rattle while he descended, and then she settled back onto the bare feather pillow. It stank. A few minutes, and someone shook the panes again coming up the stairs.

It was Sally—Sol—with sheets and a blanket. "Funky, funky, funky," he said, "but it's bigger than mine. I have a studio downstairs off the kitchen." He stood by the bed looking haggard, though he smiled. "Might as well live near the job—I have to be in the kitchen by six a.m. anyhow. Can you stand it, honey?"

"Sure."

"The renter just moved out. The plan is we clean it up and move in next week. Me and Jay."

"You mean—you and Jay? Move in?"

"Move in. Me and Jay. That's the situation."

"Okay," she said.

"Might as well take a shot. At least he's not going anywhere. He's stuck."

"So you guys all knew each other somewhere. Alhambra."

"Alhambra, USA. Jimmy burned up the life down there, huh? Fact is, there's a real coincidence going on here. I got a little crazy down there myself."

"Well," she said.

"Who's after him? Is it the cops, or is it Gambol and Juarez and all those nice people?"

"Gambol," Anita said. "Who's that?"

Sally still held the towels. Picking at the fabric with one hand. "So it's Gambol."

"I don't know. The name just sounded familiar."

"Gambol," Sally said, "just keeps coming."

"I don't think Jimmy would hang around for somebody like that."

"Then who's Jimmy hanging around for now?" He looked at Anita. "Oh. Yeah."

When Sally was gone, Jimmy came back with his duffel and their JCPenney shopping bags and set them all down beside the bathroom door. "The earthly goods."

Anita said nothing, making the bed.

Jimmy put on a phony smile and stuck his hands in his pockets and watched. "How's old Sally Fuck doing?"

"He seems nice enough."

"He's not, not nearly."

"Who's Juarez?"

Jimmy lit a cigarette.

"Or did he mean Juarez like the place?"

"Sally mentioned Juarez?" Jimmy took one drag and tossed his smoke through the bathroom door into the toilet. "Juarez is not the place. He's a guy who owns a couple dumpy clubs and porn joints. Sally disappeared two or three years ago with a whole lot of money, and there's a bounty out for his head. It wasn't Juarez's money, but Juarez is the kind of guy who collects things."

"Like bounties."

"Yeah. You're quick. Listen. Whatever you do, don't talk to Sally about the situation."

"What situation?"

"Exactly. You got it. Don't talk to him."

•

Mary understood her patient was important to Juarez. Juarez had promised her twenty thousand to get this man walking again. Juarez hadn't said what he'd give her if things went wrong.

To Mary the patient didn't look like anybody important. Long-limbed, long-faced, with a heavy brow and deep-set, melancholy eyes that made him seem thoughtful. But he was beginning to impress her as stupid. After every hypo of morphine sulfate he hopped on a cloud and held court for about thirty minutes. Apparently he'd once eaten a man's testicles.

"Juarez ate one, and I ate one. Neither one of us puked. Because when I hate somebody, my hatred is bitter till I do something horrible to soothe it."

He sat on the couch in Mary's pastel-blue bathrobe, his wounded leg laid out on the ottoman. It looked like a bloated corpse. She knew it hurt.

"I itch all over. I gotta piss. I haven't pissed in two days."

"Honey, you're on a morphine bash. You won't be able to piss till it's over."

"I know that loser," he said.

"Are you calling Juarez a loser?"

"Not Juarez. Jimmy Luntz."

She brought him the bedpan.

He gave her the finger. "Get that thing away from me."

"Just try and pee."

"I can't pee on cue."

"Ha ha."

"I like the way you laugh."

"Honey, that was fake."

In the nylon robe the patient looked ridiculous, holding his tool in his hand and steering it toward the metal pan, gazing at her contented, doped-up, expressionless. "Mary. Right?"

"Right."

"You are what we call a hefty blonde. You look about forty."

"I'm forty-four. Thirty-eight in the bust."

"Forty-four years old? That's okay. I used to like the young ones, but ever since my niece started growing a bust herself, I changed my taste. Now the young ones all look like my niece."

Mary tossed the empty ampule under the sink. "Enjoy yourself, big guy. That was the last happy hypo. After this it's just Oxycodone and Amoxicillin."

"I'm trying to straighten her out. She got arrested for shoplifting."

"Who?"

"My niece. Aren't you listening?"

"Sure. And taking notes."

"I'm trying to tell her a few things, get her lined up for the future. She says there is no future."

"Pee, or put your dick away."

"Her dad just died. My kid brother. Thirty-seven years old. Allergic reaction."

"Reaction to what?"

"Fuck if I know."

"You better find out. If it runs in the family—"

"Him and I were the last men in the family. Now it's me. If I croak, the family name is erased."

"What's the name?"

"Just call me Ernest."

"Not Ernie?"

"What do you think?"

"Okay. Ernest."

"Yeah. Okay. What about a happy ending?"

"Not dying when somebody shoots you is about as happy as it gets."

"Do you know what I mean? Like the massage girls? I mean a blow job. That's a happy ending."

"Happy for you, is all. For me it's a mouthful of fuckwad."

"What's Juarez paying you for all this medical care?"

"Enough to get four acres in Montana."

"I'll put five on top of it."

"Five what?"

"Five K."

"For a blow job?"

"For nothing. For saving my ass. Like a thank-you."

"You're welcome. Now close your pretty robe."

•

Juarez called. Gambol couldn't make sense of the conversation. Juarez said, or Gambol said, "Fucking Luntz." One of them said Fucking Luntz.

"Gambol. You there?"

"Yeah."

"Then talk. Don't just breathe. I been hearing from him time to time."

"Who?"

"Fucking Luntz. This asshole makes my stomach hurt. He refuses to behave, and he refuses to make sense. I hate him."

"Fucking Luntz."

"It's embarrassing to hate your enemy. When you're cold, that's better. Then you can move. You're more precise—you know where respect comes from? When you're precise. Gambol. Gambol."

"Yeah."

"Are you using a cell phone? What's her phone?"

"No."

"Is it a cell phone?"

"I said no."

"Fucking cell phones, you never know what with them."

"I like her."

"Mr. Gambol . . . Jesus."

"Put five K on top. That's from me."

"Definitely. Whatever you need."

"Whatever she wants."

"Sure. How doped-up are you?"

"Who?"

"Good. But not too much. Put Mary on. She there?"

"She's always here." Gambol stuck the phone in Mary's face and closed his eyes.

•

Luntz preferred shows with plenty of skin, but tonight he had no opinion. He let Anita control the remote and sat in the only chair with his legs straight out and his ankles crossed, staring at his brown socks and dipping his ashes in a coffee cup. She sat against the wall in the bed in her pin-striped pantsuit. One channel after another.

Around ten they turned in. She wore her bra and panties to bed. They lay side by side, Luntz in his boxers and T-shirt. He rested his cheek on his outstretched arm and tried conversing. She told him she felt sweaty, and she asked him to keep his distance. He tried touching her bare shoulder with his finger. His hand shook. She turned to the wall, and then she asked to have the outside half of the bed. He got up for that, found one window that wasn't stuck, and raised it three inches. Anita turned the television back on.

He put on his pants and shoes and went down the stairs.

The café was closed, but there was light in there from somewhere. He banged on the door. Turned his back and watched the road. Not one car.

Sally opened the door. "Jimmy Luntz, as I live and breathe."

Luntz said, "God. There's a lot of stars here."

"Please don't call me God. I'm a sinner like you."

"Where's Capra?"

"Zonked in his Silver Streak. I won't go in there. It smells like socks."

Luntz brought his wrist close to his face. "It's only eleven."

"You want to set a couple of chairs out back? And wrap up in blankets and listen to the river and watch the stars?"

"What for?"

"Exactly. Exactly, man."

"Sell me some booze."

Back upstairs again he stripped to his underwear while she poured a big one, not too much Sprite, and got half of it down without pausing for breath.

"You do drink like an Indian."

"Or else my pants wouldn't have come off last night, so don't complain." She lay back, raising her drink like a torch to keep it level, and slipped two fingers into the elastic of her panties and snaked them down around her thighs and ran two fingers over her mound, back and forth, and looked right at him until he was forced to clear his throat and swallow. The crushed ice sloshed in the go-cup as she finished her Popov and Sprite and set the cup aside.

The TV emitted a small steady roar. In the show a man clung to the side of a speeding train. Luntz let the TV run so he could see her by its light. All through their lovemaking Anita kept quiet, but she looked right at him. When she came, she said, "No. No. No."

•

Next morning Anita seemed morose, sitting naked on the bed's edge, staring at her clothes all bunched up together on the floor. He came out of the shower and found her like that. She didn't look at him. He sat beside her on the bed and toweled his hair and lassoed her around the shoulders with the towel, holding the ends in either hand, and she didn't seem to mind.

He studied the general moment, taking the atmospheric temperature, and let her go. "What's on TV?" he said. "I usually watch in the daytime."

"No. Really?"

"I get up late and just stay in bed and burn the daylight down."

"A night person."

"That's right, yeah. I blend in better that way."

"Not the outdoor type."

"My idea of a health trip is switching to menthols and getting a tan," he said. "I don't like push-ups, sit-ups, ex cetera. Et cetera, I mean." He'd been corrected in this several times, but always forgot.

"You're cute enough," she said, "but you got a sissy body."

"Didn't you know that?"

"What."

"That it's et cetera, not ex cetera."

"Yeah, man, I did. I just didn't feel like embarrassing you," she said, and headed for the bathroom.

When she came out he told her, "I watched you going to the shower and I almost thought I could break down crying."

"Oh," she said.

"Come here." She sat beside him, both of them naked, and he kissed her, and the temperature felt better. "I'd like to try it sober."

"Can we wait till after breakfast, when I'm not hung over?"

"Sure. Let's go downstairs. What are we having?"

"Beer."

"No problem. Day or night, Sally can fix it."

"Is he sleeping in the other guy's trailer? Who's the other guy again?"

"Capra."

"Where do they sleep? Downstairs, or in the trailer?"

"Who? Sally and Capra? They don't sleep together."

"Sally told me they're moving in together."

"Wow. No shit?"

"That's the story."

"If it's love, it's love," he said. "I had a woman I lived with off and on for—Jesus. Six years. And it was never love. And if it ain't love, it ain't love."

"I'll tell you what's love: Jimmy Luntz loves to state the obvious."

"Don't piss on my philosophy."

"I'm just hung over. And I'm scared."

"Of what?"

"You name it."

"No. You name it."

"Yesterday, today, and tomorrow. Anything else—hell, I'll spit right in its face."

"What do you mean? There's nothing else."

"See? Boy loves to state the obvious."

When they made love a while later he tasted a little beer on her breath, but she was sober. They lay together afterward, and she rested her leg over his. They watched a show on TV about the miracles of forensic science, and

Anita told him it was a bogus show. "There are six thousand unsolved murders a year in this country."

"Let's hope so," he said, and switched it off.

"What now?"

"Let's do what I always do."

"Which is?"

"Double down, honey."

"You want to try me in a different position?" The way she said it, his throat tightened and he couldn't answer.

She asked him to go on his knees by the bed—while she sat on the edge with her feet on the floor and her legs apart—and get into her that way.

It didn't work. Anita said, "You're too—"

"I'm not eight feet tall, yeah. It can't happen."

But she liked it fine the regular way and called him Daddyman and cried no, no, no when she came. He lay beside her and dried the sweat between her breasts with a corner of the bedsheet. Then to keep from asking questions he sat up and put his feet on the floor and lit a cigarette. But she touched his back with her fingers, and the question asked itself. "Why are you with me?"

"I like a bad man who hates himself. I want all the bad people to hate themselves."

"Are you bad, Anita?"

"Yes."

"Do you hate yourself?"

"Not enough."

•

Luntz kept track of the days. Today was Tuesday.

Luntz went down once around 3:00 p.m. and came back upstairs with burgers and fries and soft drinks and vodka. She made love like a drunken nun, and he liked that, but the conversation afterward was not at all aimless or relaxed. "What you really want," he told her, "is revenge."

"Yeah. I've fantasized about revenge. Do you want to hear how sick it gets?"

"No."

"The judge has the money. Or half of it at least."

"What about Hank?"

"I'll take care of Hank."

Luntz said, "You don't hide two million in a shoe. They've got it in some offshore account."

"The judge is a sick old man. When we put two guns in his face, he'll come up with it. We'll make him transfer it."

"Must be eleven felonies in that scenario."

"Unreported felonies. You can't steal stolen money. If a tree falls in the forest and nobody hears it, did it really make a sound? Fuck, no!"

Luntz said, "You're the sure shot. In my whole life, I've fired exactly one bullet."

Anita said, "I can knock bottles off a fence all day. But I'm not the guy who shot a guy."

•

Blondie sat on the ottoman, helping him with leg lifts.

"What's your name again?"

"Mary."

"How much more of this shit?"

"Till I say. Or else you'll lose muscle mass, and you'll gimp around for months."

"It looks good. I mean the sutures and all, a very professional job. Were you in a war?"

"I was on a hospital ship off Panama during that thing, and at the Army hospital in Frankfurt during the first Gulf. And I did six months in Iraq in oh-three."

"No shit. Where'd you get all the equipment?"

"Stole it. I work as a temp sometimes, in different clinics. And the hospital."

"You sell it out of your garage, or what?"

"Nope. I just like to steal things."

She helped him lie on his belly on the couch and started an alcohol rub between his shoulder blades. He told her, "Baby, don't ever stop."

"That's what they all say."

"I'm sorry if your car's ruined."

"No, man, I know gunshot wounds are bloody. I had the whole back seat and floor covered in plastic sheets all ready for you."

As he spoke, lying there under her pleasant hands, he felt his chin lifting his head up and down. "I guess this whole business is pretty fucked, huh? Guy with a hole in his leg just shows up and moves in."

"I don't mind. It's got some reality to it. Like war."

"So how did our boy talk you into this?"

"He sends me money every month."

"Why?"

"Because my attorney said so."

"You were married to Juarez?"

"I know what you think—I got fat and middle-aged and he dumped me. But no, he dumped me way before that. Then I joined the service."

She helped him ease over onto his back, and she began on his shoulders and chest.

"Are you a natural blonde?"

"None of your business," she said, "but yes, I sure am."

"How'd you get mixed up with a Mexican?"

"Hey. Mexicans are human too."

"I'm just curious. Wait," he said as she moved her hands to his legs, "you're skipping the important part."

"How well do you know Juarez?"

"We go way back."

"Not as far as me," she said. "Ever wonder why Juarez doesn't have any Mexican friends? Why he's not in with a totally Chicano gang with headbands and tattoos and all that? I mean, where's his Mexican buddies? It's because he's not Mexican. He's Jordanian. And partly Greek, I think."

"You mean Juarez is an Arab?"

"Arab, yeah. His name is Mohammed Kwa-something."

"He's a fucking Muslim?"

"What? I don't know." She put her hands lightly on his groin.

Gambol pushed her hands away, gripped the back of the couch, and hauled himself to a sitting position. "I could've called any one of a thousand guys on the phone to get my ass out of that culvert. And not one of them would've done it. Only Juarez."

She tried to close the robe for him, gave up, moved to the end of the couch, wide-eyed. "Sorry."

"Juarez is not a fucking Muslim."

"I didn't say he was. Sorry."

"Come here. I'm going to come in your face."

"Lie back down and keep the leg elevated." She stood up and gave him the finger. "You're not ready for target practice."

•

It was morning, and—according to Jimmy—Wednesday.

With her lipstick in one hand and the bottle in the other, she took two swallows of Popov, and it went down like mother's milk. Jimmy wrested it away from her and screwed the cap on and said, "No drunks in court."

She leaned into the mirror and got her lips just right. She turned to him. "I'm nervous."

"Beautiful women don't get nervous." He rested one

hand on her shoulder. "Just cross your fingers and stay calm. And don't talk fast."

"I've seen it done."

He escorted her down the stairs.

Just before she got in the car, he took out his wallet and handed her five one-hundred-dollar bills.

"Hey. No."

"Take it. You're with me now."

As she got into the Caddy, he said, "Remember"—and raised two crossed fingers. "And don't talk fast."

He shut the door for her as she turned the key. She gunned it twice. He tapped a finger on her window, and she lowered it all the way.

He put his forearms on the sill and leaned toward her and said, "Let's get it."

"For real?"

"Yeah."

"Don't say it if it isn't real."

"I've more or less done the hard part, which is gunning down a member of the gangster police force. I declare their shit null and void." His eyes were wide and his face tight with fear.

•

Mary came in from the store and set two white plastic bags of groceries on the kitchen counter. The next thing she did was light a cigarette. She wore a skirt today.

Gambol held out the classifieds and shook them at her. "Call this guy."

"Who?"

"Buy the gun. He's offering a case of ammo too, but don't take it. Is there a gun store in town?"

"How would I know that?"

"Look in the book for a gun shop. Get me some MagSafe ammo for a three-fifty-seven Magnum. They come in packs of five or six. Get me ten packs. You need me to write that down?"

"Don't strain your mind." She opened a drawer in the kitchen and found a pen and pad. Sat on the coffee table and placed her cigarette on the ashtray's edge and crossed her legs like a secretary. She had good legs. "Say again."

"MagSafe. Three-fifty-seven Magnum. Ten packs. And a box of fifty regular rounds too—the cheapest, it doesn't matter. And get me clothes, three of everything. Extra-large shirts, extra-large T-shirts. At least a forty-inch waist for the shorts. And forty-two waist and thirty-six length for the slacks. I'll reimburse you later. And shoes, jogging shoes. Eleven-E."

"It won't be the same, you without your cute robe."

He stared at her legs.

"Ernest. What are you looking at?"

"Let me ask you something. What did you think, fighting against the Arabs and knowing you used to be married to a fucking Arab? That one of them used to fuck you?"

"Hey. Arabs are human too."

Gambol ground his thumb down onto the burning ember in the ashtray and extinguished it. "And get a new robe for yourself. Get a short one."

•

Gambol examined the gun. It looked fine. When he needed to know for sure, he could take it five miles in any direction and find a place where gunshots wouldn't disturb anybody.

Mary stood before him until he noticed her. "Is this the kind of robe you had in mind?" She pinched its silk and raised the hem half an inch.

Gambol said, "Jesus Christ."

"You think Juarez would look this good in a shorty robe?"

He meant to say not a chance, but she raised the hem another two inches and scratched lightly with a fingernail high up on her thigh, and when he opened his mouth nothing came out.

She sat on the ottoman's edge and unfastened the belt of Gambol's robe, and he said, "I told you—no bedpan."

"That's not what I'm doing," she said, and knelt before him.

He watched her. She enjoyed what she was doing, he saw that. And he smelled breakfast cooking too.

She paused, and raised her face to him. "Juarez didn't pull you out of that culvert. I did."

She lowered her face to him.

Luntz unzipped the duffel bag. He laid the shotgun on the bed.

Capra didn't touch it. "Pistol grip's illegal in California."

"And smoking's illegal. Everything."

Capra ran one finger along its length. "Where'd you get it?"

"Won it in a poker game."

"Do you have evil intentions?"

"I thought I might sell it, or something."

"How much you want?"

"I don't know. I might keep it. If I knew how to use it."

Capra hoisted the gun. "Watch my thumb. See this button?" Luntz watched as Capra ran the slide back and forth repeatedly—klick-*ack*! klick-*ack*! klick-*ack*!—and eight red shells popped out one by one onto the mattress. "Well, don't travel with it loaded, for one thing. Cops frown on that shit. Anyway"—as he ran the slide back and forth again, klick-*ack*!—"that's all you need to do, right there. You hear sinister noises downstairs, just"—klick-*ack*!—"and to an intruder, that's the ugliest sound in the world."

"How do you get the shells back in?"

"Under here. You want to unload it, push this button like I showed you and run the action. And this one is your safety. Red side out means safety off. Push it in, and your trigger don't pull."

Luntz accepted the gun from his hands and slipped the shells back into the magazine one by one and made sure he had the safety on. "I think I'm considering a little move."

"Obviously."

"I'd be willing to accept some help."

"Jimmy, I'm not like that. If I was like that, my ex-wife would be dead."

Luntz replaced the gun in the duffel and zipped it shut and shoved it his whole arm's length under the bed.

"Unload it," Capra said. "You going to unload it?"

"No," Luntz said.

"Don't let Sol find out about that weapon. He's skittish."

"You always used to call Sally Sally like everybody else."

"Things change."

"If it's love, it's love."

"I'm just saying things change, man."

"Don't I know it."

Capra put his hand on the doorknob, but stood still. "Jimmy."

"Yeah."

"You've gotten quiet. I like it."

•

Juarez called. He told Gambol, "A really funny thing happened."

"I'm not in a mood for funny."

"This is a really funny thing. But it's not for this kind

of phone. This is a pay-phone-to-pay-phone kind of funny thing. Call me in ten minutes."

"I don't have any pants on."

"What?"

"I won't repeat myself."

"What are you wearing, honey?"

"Fuck you. Give me two hours. I need an hour just to get my pants on. Make it four o'clock."

"Exactly four o'clock p.m. Get some pants. Then get ready to laugh your pants off."

He did sound like an Arab.

•

She didn't know if she talked fast or slow. She forgot to cross her fingers. She didn't glance once at Hank, not once, that much she knew. That was the important thing.

Afterward, outside the courthouse, Hank gave her back the key to the house. Just walked up and handed it to her like a flower. "Babylove. Come on over. You've got a couple things at the place."

"A couple? My whole life is in that house."

"We don't have to break off contact."

"The fuck we don't. Last Friday in the Packard Room you didn't have anything more for me than Cajun chicken."

"Last Friday the last nail wasn't in."

"In my coffin?"

"Poor choice of words."

He wore a tailored charcoal suit. His shirt looked like cream.

"How much did you pay for that tie?"

"Money's no object. Not lately, Babylove."

"Do you have some formula you're working here? You call me Babylove X times and poof you're not a piece of shit?"

"I *am* a piece of shit." He put his hands in his pockets and smiled. He wasn't that good-looking. He simply had this way about him that suggested it was his party, and the human race was lucky to be his guest.

"You never let me in. You ripped off two-point-three million dollars and never mentioned it. And then you framed me for it."

He said, "Somebody has to be the designated bad guy."

"Why can't the real bad guy be the bad guy?"

"In this kind of situation, that honor goes to the cutest. You're the cutest."

"What an honor."

"The one they'll punish least. I'm not as cute as you. I know it's cold-blooded, and I'm horrible and mean, but lift your head up and take in the scenery here. Does it look like prison? It's over, and we're both standing on the street."

"Meanwhile, I pay eight hundred a month, and no job."

"Babylove. Wake up. It's over."

"Eight hundred a month for *life*. How over is that?"

"Are you staying around?"

"What do you think?"

"I'm not staying around either. Why don't we not stay around together?"

"Do I look that desperate? All I need in this world is half a tank of gas to get to the next man. And he's a better man than you."

"Don't kill me. Don't you know you can kill me, talking that way? I'm the one who's desperate."

"You lie and you lie and you lie."

"What do you want? Just tell me."

"I want to see you grovel."

"I'm groveling now. How do you like it?"

"I love it. That tie must've cost two hundred dollars."

"There's more where that came from. Why don't we share the wealth?"

She turned around and left. She didn't look back.

•

Later she drove by the house. He probably wasn't home. No reason he'd be home at two in the afternoon. But his gray Lexus sat in the driveway. The Lexus didn't mean he was home. He might be driving a second car. He could afford one. He could own eight cars by now. He could be heading a parade of newly purchased automobiles down Main Street. In her shaking hand the key chain jingled. She put the key in the lock. She swung open the door. He was home. "Babylove," he said. "I'm pouring you a drink."

Seven minutes later he went down on the floor by the bed. She said, "I like you on your knees, Daddyman."

She saw tears in his eyes.

She was weeping too. "Now beg." _____

•

Ernest Gambol proceeded into the traffic and across the street looking neither right nor left, setting his aluminum cane down hard with each step forward. The pain was good pain. Different than before.

He entered the parking lot of the Circle K. As he passed behind the Wonder Bread truck idling out front, its reverse lights flared. He struck the nearest one with his cane and shattered it. He made his way to the pay phone, where he rested his weight on both feet equally and allowed four minutes to pass. He punched the buttons and called the pay phone out front of O'Doul's.

Juarez answered. "Alhambra here."

"It's me."

"Are you ready to laugh?"

"I'm ready."

"You got your pants on?"

"Jesus Christ."

"Are you ready?"

"I said I was."

"Do you remember Sally Fuck?"

PART THREE

MARY poured some bourbon over ice and asked Gambol, "Do you want a drink?" He'd already told her twice to shut up, but she couldn't help herself.

Gambol, sitting on the couch in his boxers and Mary's blue nylon robe, said nothing. He stared at his wounded right leg, outstretched before him on the ottoman. His brow looked even heavier than usual. He kept his lips clamped together. It didn't seem possible, but maybe he was thinking.

Mary took her drink to the coffee table and sat beside him on the couch. Together they watched the final minutes of *Law & Order*. No conversation but the fraught dialogue of cops and crooks, no other sound but the ice in her glass when she sipped from it.

When the show was over, Gambol looked at his wristwatch.

Mary knelt on the floor beside the ottoman and parted the hem of his robe and examined the wound. He couldn't appreciate the work. When it came to suturing, she was better than most doctors she'd assisted. "You're healing fast, but I'm leaving those stitches in awhile. Seven days minimum for a wound to the proximal lower extremity. Ten days would be better."

He placed his hand gently on her head. She laid her cheek on his thigh and stared at his crotch. "Did I say you had one leg still working? Make that two out of three." She reached for the remote and killed the power, and he relaxed on the couch while she knelt between his splayed knees with her head going up and down.

In only a matter of seconds she sat beside him again, wiping her lips with her thumb, and said, "What's got you so excited?"

Gambol stared straight forward, stroking her hair.

She handed him his aluminum cane. "Let's see how the bad leg's doing."

He gripped the cane's head with both hands, stood up straight, and let the cane fall to the carpet. Taking uneven, quite deliberate steps, he got himself to the bedroom and turned on the light. Mary rose to join him, but he shut the door.

When he opened it again in a few minutes, Mary was still standing beside the television, and Gambol was dressed for the street, all but the footwear. A pair of black socks jutted from his shirt pocket.

He went into the bathroom, and she heard him piss a long time and flush and turn the faucet on and off. She heard him messing in the medicine cabinet, went to see—

he was emptying a tin of Band-Aids into his hand and shoving his pants pockets full of them.

She got out of his way and observed him while he behaved like a one-legged contestant in a game of Treasure Hunt, stumping around the place and collecting unrelated items. Six feet of toilet paper—bunching it into a ball in his large hand as he hobbled into the kitchen—her car keys from the magnetic hook on the door of the fridge, a Magic Marker from a kitchen drawer, and from the drawer next to the sink, his .357 Magnum and its clip-on holster and a box of rounds. Clamping the Magic Marker in his teeth like a cigar, he began loading the weapon.

Mary said, "Ernest, are you going someplace? Or maybe we?"

He took two packs of MagSafe rounds from the drawer and put one in each front pocket of his trousers and closed the drawer. He clipped the holster to his belt and slipped the gun into the holster and snapped the strap across the hammer.

Mary said, "Should I get dressed?"

He made his way back to the couch. She retrieved the cane for him, and he grasped it and sat down with considerable care and put the wounded leg on the ottoman and handed her his socks.

As she got the socks onto his feet, she said, "Let me see you work that foot. Lift your leg up and down. Not the whole leg—bend at the knee. I want to see how the knee works. Now lift your leg and dangle your foot. Is that the best you can do? You're crazy if you think you can drive. I wouldn't give you twenty minutes working the pedals."

Meanwhile he was scribbling on his jogging shoes with the Magic Marker, blacking out the reflectors on the heels and toes.

"Look," she said. "I'm here. Use me. I can deal with it when things get real. I like it."

He put both feet on the floor and began getting his shoes on. The right one obviously pained him.

"Ernest, let me help you with that." But he placed his whole hand on her head, and she felt his fingers hard against her temples. She said, "Okay, my mistake," and he released her.

He worked his foot into the shoe. With a woofing grunt, he bent at his waist and yanked tight the Velcro stays.

He went into the bedroom again, this time using the cane to walk, and came out wearing one of her sweaters, a large gray one she'd knitted herself. He pulled at its hem and covered most of the holster. Then he reached into his pocket and found a penlight no bigger than a finger and adjusted it and shone it toward her face.

She squinted at the tiny glare and said, "Works fine."

He went to the kitchen door—the door to the utility room and the garage—and she said, "The opener's clipped to the visor."

He closed the kitchen door behind him. She heard the door of her car slam and listened carefully and heard the car's door open a second time and close more softly. Then maybe once more it opened and closed, this last time so quietly she couldn't be certain.

The car's engine started, and she listened to the sound of the garage door opening and closing, and then the sound of the engine growing small out in the neighborhood, until she couldn't hear it at all. She lit a cigarette and turned on the television.

•

In the jagged silhouettes of the treetops to his left, a small glow began and followed him as he drove. In three or four minutes the moon had risen into view. A crescent moon. Muslim moon. It gave very little light.

Gambol watched the odometer. A half dozen miles along the Feather River Road, he pulled Mary's Lumina left onto the shoulder facing oncoming traffic—there wasn't any—and stopped. He pressed the window button with the meat of his hand and smelled the sharp odor of pine as the window came down. He shut off the car's engine. He heard nothing but the breeze in the evergreens.

For a midsized car, the Lumina had unusually generous leg room. Nevertheless his right leg began to throb, the discomfort pulsing in hot waves from groin to ankle. In order to keep his head clear, he'd taken no painkillers since noon.

With some difficulty he bent to remove the gun from

under his seat and opened and spun and closed the cylinder. From his back pocket he extracted a ball of Mary's toilet paper and made two small wads, soaked each in his mouth, and put one in each ear. He extended the weapon toward the open window and fired twice, paused, cranked off three more test rounds, paused a few seconds, and fired again.

He pried the spitwads from his ears and tossed them out the window, laid the gun on the passenger seat, and drove for five minutes before stopping to eject and pocket the casings and reload, this time with the MagSafe rounds. He opened his door a few inches, and by the dome light's illumination he searched for the switch that disabled it. He opened and closed the door several times in darkness.

In thirty-five minutes he'd traveled twenty-one miles farther on the winding road, and on the left, as he'd expected, he passed the restaurant. He saw lights on downstairs and one pickup truck parked on the building's near side, as he'd been promised.

A half mile beyond the site he turned the car around and cruised past it once again. On this side of the building, the ground dropped into darkness and continued toward the river.

Farther along he shut off the headlights and again turned the car around. A hundred yards short of the restaurant he stopped and lowered all four windows. He heard nothing but a steady noise he took to be that of the river.

Easing the car slowly along the left shoulder, he brought the restaurant into view and coasted to a halt, avoiding the brake lest his stop lights flare. He turned off the engine.

The darkness allowed only the most general impression of the environment—sloping, heavily treed on both sides of the building, with open ground to the rear, and then the river. The building was old enough that it seemed to have settled slightly out of plumb.

He checked his watch. Twelve-fifteen a.m. No estimation was possible of the time this would take.

From the building's shape it was clear that the upstairs was smaller than the first story. He guessed that somewhere toward the rear of the restaurant he'd find stairs going up—where, exactly, he hadn't been told. He hadn't been told how long a climb to expect. He'd been told only that the upstairs consisted of a single small apartment occupied by Jimmy Luntz.

From his pockets he dug a handful of Mary's Band-Aids. He stretched his right leg across the bench seat, sat back against the door, and applied ten of them to his fingertips one by one.

•

Jimmy Luntz stood on the landing just outside the wide-open door, finishing a cigarette under the crescent moon and listening to the washing sound of the river, not unlike the freeways he was used to. The television, tuned to MTV, lit the air of the room behind him and seemed to tug at it so that room lurched back and forth.

Now from the restaurant downstairs came a relentless basso thumping. What song? He couldn't tell. Just a jungle rhythm.

Luntz went down the stairs and around to the front and found Sally Fuck silhouetted in the restaurant's doorway, swaying like a stalk, directing music with one hand and holding a large glass in the other and singing, "Red, red wine," over and over. He pointed at Luntz. "Come on. Harmonize."

"Sell me some smokes, Sally."

"Sally who? No such Sally here."

"Sol. Sol. Sell me some smokes, Sol."

John Capra came out the door and stood scratching his beard and his belly simultaneously and said, "Fuck."

"I smell food," Luntz said.

"Ratburgers."

They went inside, and Luntz and Sally sat at the counter. All the lights were off except the light over the griddle and the light of the jukebox in a far corner. Luntz said, "I didn't know that old Wurlitzer worked."

"Some nights it never stops." Capra threw two hot dogs on the grill beside half a dozen others already frying. "You want three?"

"Just a couple."

Sally sat on the stool beside Luntz's with his back

against the counter and his legs out straight and sang through an entire Rolling Stones number. The song ended and the jukebox stood silent. On top of the jukebox lay a blackened engine part.

Sally poured his empty water glass full of red wine from a green half-gallon jug and said, "Jimmy, Jimmy, Jimmy. Where's your girlfriend?"

"She went to court."

"Night court?"

Luntz was silent.

"She looked like a natural at the wheel of that Cadillac. Anita, Anita. Nuthin' sweetah. She's been gone three days. You figure she's coming back?"

"I try not to figure."

"I figure you just lost a Cadillac, Jimmy."

Capra set down on the counter a basket of fries still dripping a little grease and said, "Anita Desilvera is one good-looking woman."

Sally said, "Wouldn't you just love to suck on her stank —you whore?"

"Did you hear a car earlier?" Luntz said.

Sally said, "Jimmy, Jimmy, Jimmy, she's not coming back," and dropped a french fry into his mouth like a worm. "A glass of wine for the cocksman."

Luntz said, "You got club soda?"

Capra went to the cooler and brought him a can, popping the top as he set it down on the counter. "You still got that funny stomach?"

"Same one."

"A shot of wine wouldn't hurt it," Sally said, and raised his glass.

Luntz said, "I don't like the way you're staring at me."

Sally said, "It's just because the light comes from behind you, man."

Capra slammed three plates down on the counter, *bang*, *bang*, *bang*, and said, "You are really drunk."

Sally said, "Drunk is good tonight, my melodious little cum-swallower," and shoved a frankfurter into his mouth.

Luntz said, "What else do you do around here for fun?"

"When the others get back from Bolinas," Capra said, "we'll see a little more action."

"When is that?"

"They'll start turning up tomorrow. We got half a dozen, sometimes a dozen people living here."

Sally said, "Bikers."

"Bikers are my people, Sol."

"They're just like everybody else around here. Around here," he told Jimmy, "it's the great outdoors. They all subscribe to *Dog and Woman* magazine." Again Sally was squinting at Luntz. "You look like a man without much to live for."

"What the fuck does that mean?"

"Leave him alone, Sol." Capra stopped scraping the grill and ate three hot dogs in ninety seconds and went back to scraping. "You still play the sax?"

"Jimmy loves sax."

Capra ceased his movements at the grill. He didn't turn around. "Shut up, Sally."

"My name is Solomon Fuchs, honey, and you can call me Sol."

"People tell me I look like Art Pepper," Luntz said, "but I don't blow as good as he does."

"Beg *pardon*?"

"Nobody blows like Art."

"I never said anybody did."

"Well, I played some."

Sally's interest seemed authentic. "What about Art?"

"Actually, I keep forgetting. Art's dead."

"Okay."

"But his music lives on. I don't care if that's a sweet thing to say. It's a true sweet thing."

"Sure," Sally said. "And when was the last time you played professionally?"

"Me? I don't know. I don't even have a sax. I'm kind of in hock."

"When was the last time?"

"An actual gig? For money? Well, an actual *gig* . . . What is this, anyway," Luntz said, "Gamblers Anonymous?"

Sally ate half his second hot dog and shoved the rest of his meal aside and said, "So name me two things you've got to live for."

Capra said, "Sol. Don't continue this shit."

"Don't be a hairy-headed biker with greasy knuckles."

Capra leaned over the counter and seized Sally's chin

and got close to his face and said, "Quit ragging on him like a bitch."

Sol stared at Capra with a kind of fearful hatred. "I get on the back of a motorcycle, all I think about is getting off."

Capra splayed his fingers and released Sally's chin. "He gets bitchy. He made his bed and now he doesn't like it."

Sally said, "We're all in the same bed."

"Only two of us," Capra said.

"Jimmy, Jimmy, Jimmy. I understand you shot Gambol."

Capra put his hands on the counter and stared down at them. Sally laughed. Phony laughter.

Capra said, "Jesus, Jimmy."

"These fries are good," Luntz said.

Capra gathered up the plates and went to wiping down the counter with a rag. After a while he said, "When you turned up from outer space, I figured, you know—bad debts."

"I do have bad debts."

"So the Caddy you loaned your girlfriend. And the shotgun. Jesus. So Juarez is after you."

"I just wanted to see if I could do it."

"You offed Gambol and stole his shit?"

"He's all right. I hear he's recuperating."

"He's not dead? Fuck me. That means Juarez *plus* Gambol."

"What shotgun?" Sally said.

"Shut up for two fucking seconds," Capra said, "just for two seconds, all right? I've got some serious shit to say." Luntz and Sally were quiet, and he said, "I need you out of here tomorrow, Jimmy."

"Bye-bye, Jimmy."

"That's quick notice."

"It is what it is."

"Give him another day," Sally said. "Give him till Sunday."

"I'd appreciate it," Luntz said.

"Noon Sunday. Not one fucking minute later. I'm serious. You didn't lay it out, man. I didn't realize your shit stank this bad."

"I guess we all stink pretty bad, huh?"

"Whatever that means," Capra said.

"Well, the only thing I knew about you was—'Feather River.' I just knew you were hid. I didn't know you were mixed up in Sally's thing."

Sally said, "Do you ever speak in anything but double meanings?"

"Okay, Sally," Luntz said, "confession time. How much did you get away with down there? Weren't you an accountant for the syndicate or something?"

"I was a public information man for the Cooperative Agriculture Board, and I was a bagman for them on one single occasion. Of which I took instant crazy advantage."

"How much in the bag?"

"Three hundred and eighty-six thousand. The whole

idea"—pointing at Capra—"was his idea. And now it's happily ever after. A biker bar in the Himalayas."

"One place is as good as another," Capra said. And to Luntz he said: "Sunday."

"Three eighty-six? Wow. Got any left?"

"Oodles," Sally said. "Let me put you in a Jaguar."

"Noon," Capra said.

"Sell me some vodka to go. And some smokes."

"Noon, Sunday." Capra turned off the blower above the griddle and headed past the coolers toward the back room, saying nothing more, and Luntz was left alone with Sally Fuck, who stirred the wine in his glass with one of his long fingernails and said, "Juarez finds whoever he looks for. And Gambol eats their balls."

"Man," Luntz said, "I really don't like the way you talk."

"Anyway, according to the autopsy, Cal from Anaheim had no balls on his corpse."

"That's a legend."

"Soon to be the legend of Jimmy Luntz." Sally wasn't drinking his wine at all. Just stirring it and tasting the drops on his fingernail. "She was a beautiful Indian maiden. It's like a song."

"Kiss my ass, Sally. I need a pack of Camels."

"I'm terribly sorry. We're closed." But Sally got up to fill the order.

"And a half pint of Popov."

"Yeah. And what if she did come back? What are you going to do with that one?"

"Get her drunk."

•

Inside the restaurant, the last small light went off. The moon had climbed higher and was no longer visible to Gambol through the car's front window. Nearly 2:00 a.m., nearly fourteen hours without Oxycodone. As pain burned off the fog in his thoughts, a detail he'd overlooked rose into view.

He possessed no kind of tool for dealing with the restaurant's door. No idea how he'd get past the threshold.

He rifled the glove box. An armrest folded down in the middle of the seat, and he looked in its hutch. He found nothing to help him.

He holstered his gun and gathered up his cane and the car keys and opened the door and stood outside the car, shutting the door not quite completely, and made his way around to the rear of the vehicle. The trunk's lid unlocked with a click and a sigh. He raised it six inches, and a bulb came on within. He bent to glance inside—a spare, a jack, and two prongs of a four-pronged lug wrench—and with the weight of two fingertips he shut it. A wrench with lug ends wouldn't help. He needed a pry.

Standing by the car in the frail moonlight, he closed

his eyes and took several even breaths, beginning each from the diaphragm, filling and emptying his lungs.

He headed for the restaurant.

Halfway to the entrance he took a short detour to examine the pickup truck parked beside the building. The cargo bed was bare, recently swept. He continued toward the driver's side of the cab and saw, on the dash, all by itself, a large screwdriver with a foot-long shaft. He leaned his cane against the front wheel well and cupped a hand against the driver's window glass to shine his penlight within. It was an old Ford with novelty death's-heads for locks, pinpoint eyes of red glass. The doors weren't locked.

He eased the door toward him an inch, another—the dome light didn't function, but the door's bushings were shot, and it gave out a sharp croak as he opened it. He paused to stand up straight and listen. Only the river. The restaurant stayed dark. Without further disturbance to the door's position, he reached inside for the implement.

With this gift scabbarded in his belt he moved toward the restaurant's entrance, where he propped his cane beside the door, unsnapped his holster, and tried the doorknob. Locked.

He cupped his hand and shielded the light and ran it around the door's base and top and edges. Dead wasps and dead flies littered the threshold. The hinges lay inside, inaccessible. The lock was not a deadbolt. He pried between the lock and the jamb until the door gave sideways and the bolt came free of its housing. Pushing gently with the flat of his palm, he opened the door wide. The hinges made no sound. He retrieved his cane and gripped it hard as he stooped to lay the screwdriver on the porch.

He entered the restaurant. His penlight's beam threw up tables and chairs, and he threaded his way among them, heading generally to his right and toward the rear, where the stairs must be. As he reached the windows in the far wall he switched off his penlight and was able to see well enough to continue alongside them, skirting a round-shouldered jukebox with an old camshaft balanced on top of it. In the far corner he found two doors side by side. He tried his penlight briefly—a figure with a barbell on one door and on the other a figure with monstrous tits.

He ran the light around the molding at the base of the wall, as far as its beam would reach—no other door.

As he headed for the counter and the kitchen area, he heard a voice from exactly there, muffled by a wall, and another voice, also muffled. He unholstered the gun, set his cane on a chair, and walked as quickly as he could toward the sound. The lights behind the counter came on. A man in jeans stood some fifteen feet away with his right hand raised to the wall switch. Gambol fired two rounds, and before he could get off a third the man collapsed like a sack out of sight behind the counter.

Gambol continued to the counter and leaned over it as far as he could. The man lay motionless in the narrow space between the counter and the stove, shirtless and barefoot, facedown. Gambol took aim, holding the weapon with both hands, took note of his breathing, and in the space between his out breath and in breath squeezed the trigger carefully. The head broke open. He turned away.

Someone was shouting, but he couldn't hear the words. He turned again with his weapon and saw no one and turned away and found his cane and walked to the door and out into the night.

He had thirty yards of open space to make across the parking lot and then an equal distance along the roadside to the car, but when he reached the roadside he'd be hidden by trees. In his left hand he held the gun. With his right he gripped the cane's handle. He stiffened his right arm and right leg and marched as swiftly as he could. As he passed the pickup truck, sounds followed him, his hearing still blurred by the shock of gunfire. Footsteps, possibly, down the far side of the building, and footsteps on gravel, and then a sharp, clear sound—klick-*ack*!—that meant he hadn't moved fast enough.

•

Luntz assumed Anita was back. He heard a loud backfire. The Caddy shouldn't be doing that. And another—identical.

One is a backfire. Two is a gun.

He fell to the floor and reached under the bed for the duffel bag that held the shotgun. Rather than pulling it to him, he found himself floundering toward it under the bed. Lying on his side, he clutched the duffel to his chest and ran his hand along its length and touched the zipper. He felt capable of nothing else.

Another shot downstairs.

He put his knee to his chest and a foot against the wall and shoved himself and the duffel out from under the low bed, and his bones turned to rubber bands as he tried to stand. He rose only as far as his knees and was barely able to hoist the bag onto the bed. He jerked the zipper one way and another until it gave in the right direction. Stood up in a room tilted sideways, gripping the barrel and dangling the shotgun, aware mainly of an unbelievable trembling weakness in his legs.

He opened the door and stood ouside at the top of the stairs, turning the shotgun in his hands until he held the pistol grip. He pushed the safety button and cocked the gun—klick-*ack*!—and took a step, and his feet slipped out from under him, and he viewed, overhead, a crescent moon and several stars in a black sky as he bumped down the stairs on his spine, feeling no physical sensation at all. His feet found a purchase, and he stood and wobbled down the remaining steps and onto the earth and clambered toward the building's corner, going down several times onto one or the other knee. As he rounded the building, he pulled the trigger. His ears and his hands seemed to explode with the force, but he had hold of the weapon still, and cocked it again. He saw who he was shooting at—someone moving past the pickup at the building's other end.

Luntz chased his target as far as the road's shoulder. Now the man was hopping toward a car. Luntz raised the gun level with his shoulders and pointed and fired again —numb up his right arm and deaf in his right ear. The man jumped and turned and fell, then he pushed himself up on one hand, then onto his knees, both arms extended together. Luntz turned and flung himself to the ground, hearing gunshots, and his senses ceased functioning. When the darkness and silence ended he was over the side of the hill and standing behind the building and hearing the river, and now his senses were sharp, precise. He heard a car's door slam. Heard the car's ignition. Next he was standing in front of the restaurant again, cocking the gun's action and pulling the trigger until the gun was empty. He saw the car's taillights blink out down the road among the trees.

He was shaking, every muscle quivering. The breath shoved itself in and out of his lungs. He turned the weapon this way and that. When he touched its barrel, someone said, "Jesus!" and he wondered who was talking, and they said, "Fuck!" and he realized it was himself.

In the restaurant behind him, the lights came on. He saw small cylinders in the gravel at his feet. He had no shoes on. Only socks. To his knowledge, he hadn't hit a thing.

He heard a siren—growing nearer, louder—but it was the wail of a human voice.

The restaurant's door stood open. He went through it shouting, "Hey, hey, hey—" He didn't know why.

Sally Fuck rose up from behind the counter, wailing like a siren and wringing blood from his hands.

•

Sally came around the counter and sat on a stool and held his head in his gory fingers, his whole frame trembling.

Luntz said, "Is he dead?"

Sally raised his face. It looked like a gargoyle's, sick and shining. He laughed, and then he sobbed so hard the spit flew from his throat.

Luntz said, "What now?"

No answer.

"Sally—Sol. Sol. What now, man?"

"I don't know."

Luntz laid the shotgun on the counter and leaned over it to look at John Capra. Sally had tried to turn him over, evidently, and smeared Capra's blood in a swath across the floor. The face was turned toward the stove. The back of the head had been scooped away and flung against the oven's door. Luntz watched for movement. If somebody stared hard enough, Capra would move.

"We have to take care of this," Sally said.

"Fine. I mean—fine," Luntz said. "God. Oh, man." A lot of ideas hammered at his head, most of them having to do with Capra coming suddenly alive.

Sally swung around on his stool and got his feet under him. He started for the back. "We need a pick and a shovel."

"Gloves," Luntz called after him. "Do you have any gloves?" He stood staring at his hands. The thumb on the right one was mottled red and blue and swollen at the joint—sprained by the shotgun's recoil, maybe broken. He searched his nerves for some sensation of pain, felt none. He needed to go upstairs and get his shoes on, but he couldn't form a plan for doing it.

•

Mary had left a couple windows open and smoked whenever the impulse came. She held the ashtray in her lap and watched a desperate woman selling fourteen-carat jewelry on TV without a script to help her. By 1:00 a.m. Mary no longer heard even an occasional vehicle in the neighborhood.

Around three, a car cruised by. She turned the set off. The garage door rumbled. She heard a door open and close inside the garage, and then the car's trunk lid. She stubbed out her cigarette.

Gambol labored through the door into the kitchen and replaced the revolver in the counter drawer, took a jug of milk from the refrigerator, and drank several deep swallows from it before shutting it away again.

Leaning heavily on his cane with every step, he came and sat beside her on the couch and lifted his bad leg with both hands and dumped it across the ottoman. In the middle of sitting back, he paused. "What I don't understand about the whole thing," he said, "is when the Twin Towers went down, why didn't we just nuke the fuck out of those bastards and turn that whole Muslim desert to glass?" He sat all the way back and took one long breath and released it slowly.

"Hooray," Mary said, "he talks."

"A thousand atom bombs don't matter," he said, "if you don't have the sense to push the button."

She helped him draw the sweater over his head, and then she helped him with his shoes and his pants and boxers, saying only "Here" and "Lift a little" and "How's that?" The sweater's left elbow was ripped and dirty, also the left pants leg from hip to cuff. The wound on his right leg looked fine. He hadn't torn the sutures.

He said, "The mirror on your car is broken."

"Did it come loose?"

"The sideview mirror. The glass is broken."

"Somebody hit it?"

"Fuck if I know."

"Do I want to ask what you've been doing?"

"That's always a mistake."

"Okay."

She opened a fresh box of swabs and cleaned the light abrasions on his left hip and elbow with rubbing alcohol and disinfected the area around the right leg's mended bullet wound and finished by wiping at the grime on his fingers.

"Mind your own business," he said. "That's never a mistake."

"I kind of feel like you are my business."

"Maybe in other ways."

"What ways?"

"The various ways. You know."

She gathered up the dirty swabs in both hands and took them over to the kitchen sink. "Do you want some more milk or anything?"

"Sure. Thank you."

She tossed the swabs in the bag reserved for medical trash, and brought him milk in a clean glass. He took it from her hands and closed his eyes and sipped. "Well," she told him, "if you can run around and fall on your face, maybe you're well enough we could sleep in the same bed."

She watched him closely, and when his eyelids came up he was already staring at her face. "I don't know if I'm ready to . . . whatever."

"Let's go to bed," she said, "and maybe I could earn another five K."

"You're charging me five for every single blow job?"

"Really I'd just like to sleep with you."

"Yeah," he said, and his eyelids came down. "Fuck, yeah. I'm tired."

•

Luntz didn't know why he was the one driving the pickup. He sat in the driver's seat covered with Capra's blood and holding the shotgun in his lap and saying, "Wow. Wow. Wow." Sally sat in the passenger's seat hugging himself, leaning forward, sitting back, leaning forward, saying, "Fuck. Fuck. Fuck."

"Sally. I think I left the door open. The restaurant. The front door, man."

"Fuck the door. Fuck the door. Fuck the door."

Sally didn't say where to go, and Luntz didn't ask. He drove toward higher ground, away from any part of the world he'd already seen. Sally rolled down his window. He rolled it up again. He said, "Turn on your headlights."

"What? Jesus, I can see in the dark." Luntz's left hand scrabbled over the dashboard. "Adrenaline." He found the knob and pulled it. The road came up in front of him like an amber wall. "What the fuck is Gambol doing in my world?"

Sally said, "Jay, Jay, Jay, Jay, Jay." He had his cheek against the rear window and the fingers of one hand splayed on the glass.

"Will you stop crying, goddamn it?"

"We're all crying. You are too."

"The fuck I am." Luntz drew a long stuttering breath. He clenched his stomach and tightened his grip on the wheel and drove straight ahead. He tasted snot in his mouth.

"There's a car following us," Sally said. "Back there. With one high beam busted."

"Maybe it's a bike," Luntz said, and Sally said nothing. Luntz floored it, got around a bend, and U-turned so quickly he could hear the tools and probably Capra's body sliding across the cargo bed. Facing back the way they'd come, he floored it again, but he hadn't downshifted, and he killed the engine.

The vehicle came at them, went past, kept going.

They sat in the silent truck in the middle of the lane, both breathing hard. Sally wept. Luntz lit a Camel. "I knew it would be like this," he said. "I knew I could never handle this shit." He turned the key and rammed the gearshift and pumped the clutch and ground it into gear and wrestled with the wheel until they were heading uphill again.

Sally hocked repeatedly and spat several times onto the floor. He sat up straight with his hands on his knees. His breathing came under control. Sally said, "So this was Gambol?"

The grade steepened. Luntz yanked at the gearshift and found second.

"Yeah, it was Gambol."

"You cunt. You fucking cunt."

"Who are you talking to? Gambol isn't here, Sally. The fucker can't hear you."

"I'm talking to you, you cunt, you fucking cunt. He wanted you."

"Who? Gambol? He didn't know I was here. How would he know? He was after you, Sally."

"You fucking cunt. Maybe that Indian bitch told him. She told him. She snitched."

"Anita doesn't know a soul in Alhambra. Not one swinging dick."

"It was that cunt of yours."

"Anita never heard of Alhambra. She thought Alhambra was the name of a prison." Luntz pounded open the wing window and slipped his cigarette out into the wind, and it flew away in a shower of sparks. He didn't ask where to go. He just kept going.

·

The crescent moon lay directly overhead, and on such a night the river's swollen surface resembled the unquiet belly of a living thing you could step onto and walk across.

Anita stood in the darkness by the water, her head high and her shoulders back, and stared at the shape standing across the river from her.

Anita went onto her knees and spooned to her face four swallows of water with her left hand, and the shape across the water did the same. Now they knelt across from one another, the river between.

For half an hour she didn't move. Her knees, her calves, her hips, all burning. She did not take her eyes from the one across the river.

The last two nights in this spot had been chilly. This night too. The backs of her hands, her cheeks, her lips had been chapped by the wind.

When she got to her feet, the knees of her pants were frayed and bits of gravel clung to the fabric, but she didn't brush them clean or in any other way distract her focus from the figure kneeling on the opposite bank.

The dark shape across the water grew elongated, also standing.

They faced one another with the Feather River in between. In two or three more hours they would kneel again and drink.

•

Luntz pulled the flashlight from Sally's hands and gave it a shake and fiddled with the switch.

Sally grabbed at it. Luntz let it go. Sally banged its head on the dashboard.

"It's junk."

Sally dropped it onto the floor and stomped it twice, saying, "It's dark—it's dark!"

"We'll use the parking lights." Luntz pulled the knob, and tree trunks materialized before them in an orange glow.

They went to the back of the truck. Sally let down the tailgate and took the pickaxe and the shovel by their ends and dragged them out, letting the shovel fall. Luntz snatched the cuffs of Capra's jeans with both hands and pulled. "Help me get him out. Ah, God. His pants are coming down."

Sally said, "Jesus' bloody *nail* wounds, man. Leave him

alone." A few yards in front of the truck, Sally rolled aside a chunk of log and kicked away dead branches to make a bare enough spot and hacked at the earth with the pickaxe, hunched over, walking backward, saying, "Jesus' bloody fucking *punctures*, man."

"How deep?"

"We need four feet. Four and a half. If we do this right we can get it done in two hours. I'll break it up, and you dig it out, then I break up another layer. You work one end, I'll do the other, then we switch. I dug miles of ditches at Chancellor Farm."

"Where's that?"

"Near La Honda. Hah! In the hills. Hah! Reformatory. Hah!" Sally stopped talking and only slung the point of the pickaxe at the ground in front of him, saying, "Hah!" with every blow. In a minute he tossed his shirt aside and pulled his T-shirt over his head and wound it around the pick's handle and said, "Protect your hands," and Luntz stripped to the waste and bandaged the handle of his shovel and plunged its point into the dirt.

They worked without need of a pause. Luntz felt able to dig until his hands wore away or he struck the earth's molten core. Each time the shovel hit a stone he went to his knees in the hole and clawed it out and tossed it, no matter how big it was, many yards into the brush.

"Who's that? Who *is* it?"

"Just coyotes."

"*Just?*"

"Dig. Dig. Dig."

Sally hacked at dirt with the pickaxe as if he were going at some monster's face. "This is insane. This is insane. This is insane." Luntz joined in and they chanted together, "This is insane, this is insane, this is insane."

When they couldn't work any more from outside the hole, they took it in shifts, one resting by the edge while the other stood at the bottom and gouged. A change came to the darkness, not exactly daylight. Luntz craved water, but they'd brought none. During his rests the sprain in his right hand throbbed and burned. While he dug he felt nothing.

Sally stopped and said, "Enough, enough, that's enough." He stood in a hole up to his armpits.

Luntz helped him out and they climbed into the bed of the pickup and scooted Capra's corpse to the rear and jumped off again. Capra lay on the tailgate with his arms above his head and one leg dangling. He still had a face, but it didn't look like Capra, and the back of his head was gone. "You take that end," Luntz said, coming around Sally to wrap Capra's ankles in his arms, and Sally locked his elbows in Capra's armpits and took Capra's halved head against his chest, and they hauled the corpse around to the front of the truck and without discussion rolled Capra into his grave and buried him.

Sally collapsed beside the mound and lay on his hip, breathing hard and running his fingers over the churned earth. "When was the last time you talked to him?" he asked Luntz. "What day?"

"Me?"

"What was the last thing he said to you?"

"I don't know. You were there. He asked me how many hot dogs I wanted."

"No, no, man—something that meant something."

Luntz tried to remember. He stood up and rubbed at the muscles of his back, below the ribs. "He told me I've gotten quiet, and he said he liked it."

"Yeah." Sally laid his hand on the grave and got to one knee.

"Sally, hand me that shovel."

"It's called a spade."

Sally extended the spade's handle, and Luntz took it in both hands and said, "I can subtract, Sally," and hit him with the flat of it as hard as he could.

Sally clutched the side of his head with both hands and fell backward with his calves under him.

Luntz said, "Who told Juarez where I was?"

Sally scurried on his back like a spider, hopping, scrabbling, the blows missing, Luntz swinging anyway—"Who told Juarez—Who told Juarez—Who told Juarez?"—until Luntz's strength died, and he stopped swinging. To keep upright he leaned on the shovel. "It wasn't me, and it wasn't him, and it wasn't her. So it was you. And how did you know I shot Gambol? Juarez told you, that's how."

Sally had rolled onto his side. "That Indian bitch told me."

"Bullshit."

Sally got to his hands and knees and tried to rise and gave up. He was weeping and spitting out blood. "This is Friday, Friday, Friday."

"So what?"

"It was set up for *tomorrow* night."

"They don't come on the night they say."

"Why the fuck not?"

"Because there's always a snitch. Like you."

Sally crawled as far as the grave and put his hands on the pickaxe as if he were talking to it. "I just wanted to get us *out* of here. It doesn't have to be Alhambra."

"So you snitched to Juarez. You made a deal, is that it? And look at the shit we're in."

"LA—fuck, I don't care—*East* LA. Fine, I'll live in a trailer that smells like socks. Just put it in a *city*."

"Well," Luntz said, "you sure got Jay out."

Sally stood upright on the grave and whirled like an eerie batter at home plate, and Luntz watched the pickaxe drifting toward him until the top of the crescent struck him in the belly. He doubled, sat on his ass, and said, "What?" as the back of his head hit the ground. Sally leapt onto him and straddled Luntz's midriff and got his fingers tight around Luntz's throat and locked his arms straight, and Luntz felt him bearing down. Luntz's vision turned a brilliant brown, then a mellow purple, then a beautiful color he'd never seen before in which he had everything he needed and all the time in the world to decide what came next. He gripped the wrists of the hands choking him and removed the hands as easily as if he were taking off a sports jacket and held them out at arm's length while Sally breathed and Sally's spit dripped down into his face. Luntz's body took in great breaths of air, but Luntz himself was somewhere else without any need of air. Sally struggled backward, trying to get loose of Luntz's grip. Luntz released him.

He heard the truck's door open and close. Luntz got up slowly but without any effort. Sally came toward him with the shotgun. Luntz watched him with only peace in his heart.

"It isn't loaded."

"Want to bet?" Sally's head and shoulders whipped like a dancer's—klick-*ack*!—and he directed the gun at Luntz.

"How much?"

"Fucking Luntz. You'll bet on anything."

As Luntz walked toward Sally, he heard the tiny click of hammer on pin in the empty gun.

Sally handed the weapon over and Luntz tossed it into the truck through the window and got in and turned the engine over and cut on the headlights.

"I can't walk from here!"

"It's downhill all the way."

Sally stood in the headlights with his hand raised before his eyes. Luntz backed the truck up slowly to a spot where he could turn it around, and left him.

Luntz thought they'd taken the only road in, but now he came to a fork and without slowing down took the way that looked less rutted, and soon another fork, and now he had no idea where he was. Somewhere between himself and the river he'd find the main road, that's all he knew. As long as he didn't get turned around entirely, he was all right. He looked at his watch—it was scabbed with soil and clotted blood. He spat and polished it against his pants leg. The dial said 4:00 a.m., but its face was smashed.

The morning was bright and he'd seen miles of dirt byways before he found the paved one and turned downhill toward the restaurant.

•

Mary's cell phone started beeping, and Gambol opened his eyes and said, "Fuck him," and when it stopped beeping he and Mary went back to sleep, and when it beeped again he reached over for it and found the button and said, "Fuck you."

Juarez said, "You didn't call."

"How did you like the moon?"

"What moon?"

"Did you see the moon last night?"

"I'm in Alhambra. There's no moon. Did you accomplish a certain errand?"

"Accomplish? On what information? Fucked-up information."

"You're saying no. Things aren't complete."

"No. Just maybe the other guy."

"The person with the lady's name."

"Right. I never found any stairs. Where were the stairs?"

"Okay. New plan. Don't look back."

"No. Where were the fucking stairs?"

"It's in the past. We move on. We take care of this another way."

Gambol said, "I never found any stairs," and tossed the phone against the wall across the bedroom. Beside him, Mary stirred but seemed to be asleep. Probably pretending. Gambol closed his eyes.

He dreamed he was skiing down a slope stark naked before a crowd of sideliners, freezing cold but with a large, friendly hard-on. When he woke he found he'd thrown the covers off, and he was still cold, and his large friend was still with him.

He pulled off his boxers with one hand and gripped Mary's shoulder with the other, and as he nuzzled his groin against the backs of her thighs she turned his way with her eyes closed, and she smiled.

"The last twenty-four hours have been nothing but fucked," he told her as she opened her eyes. "The next twenty-four hours start right now."

•

Something came at Anita in the darkness, maybe the head-light of a train, but it was only the door to the waking world. As she drifted toward the door, it banged open. Jimmy stood framed in it, pointing a shotgun at her.

Lying on her back on the bed, she pushed herself up onto her elbows. Her thoughts dragged behind, and even as she stared at him she said, "Who's there?"

He shut the door and locked it. "Where were you?"

She tried to remember.

He threw the shotgun onto the bed and lifted his duffel bag from the floor and slammed it down beside her. "Where have you been since Wednesday?"

"Down by the Feather River."

"The Feather River's right out the back door."

"A different part. My part."

"For two days? Three days?"

He started snatching red cylinders from the duffel and slipping them into the shotgun.

She managed to swing her legs around and get her feet on the floor. "Please don't do that."

"It's empty."

"Then leave it empty."

"Why?"

"Because I don't want to be in a room with you and me and a loaded gun."

"Your gun's loaded." Now he took a rusty church key from the refrigerator door. His actions made no sense to her. He said, "Right? You have your gun?"

"Yeah. Yes."

He gripped one of the shells, pried an end of it open with the church key, and spilled a lot of ball bearings onto the mattress. "There's ten—eleven—fuck. Where do they go? Where do they go when you shoot the fucking *gun*?"

He put the shotgun in the duffel and started to zip it and paused, putting his hand to his mouth.

"When did you start sucking your thumb?"

"It hurts." Jimmy looked all around as if his thoughts were attacking him. "We have to go."

"I can't move."

"What?"

"I'm tired. And you're all dirty. You're filthy. You look like a farmer."

"So do you. Were you sleeping under a bridge?"

"I didn't sleep."

Jimmy stood in the bathroom door and looked at the mirror and said, "Jesus."

Sitting on the bedside, she let her head hang.

"Open your eyes." He gripped her by the chin. "Here's the plan. You shower for two minutes. I'll find us some clothes downstairs. Then I'll shower for two minutes."

"Why are you crying?"

"I'm not crying. Get in the shower."

"Jesus Christ, Jimmy, there's snot on your face."

"Let's go, let's go, let's go."

She stepped under the shower and would have stayed forever, but the bulb in the ceiling blew, and in the dimness under the falling water she thought she saw fireflies clambering from the drain and coming at her face, and she left the stall quickly. She lay on the mattress without looking for a towel and didn't realize she was falling asleep until something woke her.

Jimmy stood over her in a pair of jeans too short for his legs and too wide for his waist. "Move, honey." He tossed her a bundle of flannel and denim, and she dressed in jeans and a lumberman's shirt while he jerked her this way and that, trying to help her, and at the same time babbling math:

"We have ten percent of a plan. We go to see the judge. We take his half. That's half a million plus for each of us. We put it in two accounts and go in two separate directions. You can deal with your husband or not—that's later. I'm out of that one."

"These pants won't stay up."

"Use my belt. Where's your purse? Just give it to me." He yanked the shotgun from the duffel. "Okay. We're gone."

"Gone where?"

"There's no way to go," he said, "but the way we're going. I know how it ends, but there's no other way."

"Why?"

"Because Gambol did a bad thing. Let's go."

On the stairs down, Jimmy turned to her and said, "What about your shoes?"

"I don't need shoes." She got past him on the stairs.

"Don't you have shoes?"

"I've got feet." She passed the door to the restaurant. It stood wide open.

"Not the Caddy," Jimmy said. "The truck." Her bare feet changed course and took her to the truck.

"In. In. In."

Jimmy tossed the shotgun on the floorboards at her feet. He still held her purse. He took the Caddy's keys from it and threw the purse in her lap, shut the door in her face and went over to the Caddy and slapped the keys down on the vinyl roof.

As he climbed into the seat beside her he said, "Make it easy for the next owner." He leaned wearily against the steering wheel as he started the truck.

•

Gambol woke to the smell of food. Daylight leaked around the curtains into the room. Mary's cell phone, he saw, had returned to its charger on the nightstand. He took it in his fist and rubbed his eyes with the back of his hand and said, "Fuck."

He called O'Doul's, and a woman answered: "Dooley's. What."

"Juarez. That's what."

"The name is not familiar."

"Get Juarez. It's Gambol."

"He's not here."

"I said this is Gambol. Get him."

"He's really not here. He went north."

"North where?"

"North. That's all he said."

"When did he leave?"

"I don't know. Real early."

"Who's with him?"

"The Tall Man."

"Nobody else?"

"Just the Tall Man. Isn't that enough?"

He went out to find Mary in the kitchen in her shorty robe, standing over a fry pan with a cigarette jutting from her lips, humming a tune. "Steak and eggs," she said, "and guess what? Champagne."

"Juarez is coming up."

"Up where?"

"Up here."

"Shit. Here? Shit."

"Yeah. And the Tall Man."

"Is that monster still with him?"

"That monster's always been with him."

"Was he always like that? Born like that?"

Gambol said, "You mean tall?"

Mary laughed as if nothing was funny. "How did his face get like that?"

Gambol looked at the bloody hunks sizzling in the pan and said, "I'm not hungry."

•

Luntz pushed it hard, making sure he heard the tires on every curve. If a cop lit him up, he'd steer it off a cliff.

"You brush against these people, you know? Just brush up—and it's an electric thing, you get some juice from it, you feel like you've got some balls, but—these people are hard."

She didn't answer. He gave her shoulder a shake. "No curiosity? Don't you want the news? Capra's dead. Gambol blew his head off."

"In a hundred years we're all dead."

"Did you ever know anybody who got murdered?"

Beside him she was white and pale. "The dead come back. Death isn't the end."

"Let's be optimistic," he said, "and assume that's bull-shit."

"At night you can see them standing across the river."

"That sounds like DTs." He reached for the pocket in his too-large flannel shirt—Capra's maybe, or Sally's—and handed her the half pint of vodka. "Have a party."

She unscrewed the cap. "If you know the crossing

place," she said, "you can block their way." She looked like a child in an older brother's clothes. She turned the bottle up and wrapped her lips around its neck.

Three bikers passed, coming up the other way. Then two more traveling side by side. "Must've got an early start from Bolinas. We got out just in time." Half a minute later, a whole pack—seven, eight, nine, Luntz couldn't count.

He tried the radio and spun the dial until he hit some music, any music, not even real music—country music. News came on, and Anita slapped at the knobs until it went away.

"Are we in range? Where's your cell phone?"

"I don't know."

"Look in your purse. Let me have it. Don't just stare at it. Fuck. Call information."

"Do you want it or not?"

"Get the number for O'Doul's Tavern in Alhambra." Luntz grappled for his cigarettes and found one left in the pack. It was ripped in the middle and streaked with dirt. He managed to keep it lit through two drags before he tossed it.

Anita said, "It's dialing."

He wrested the phone from her hand as a woman answered: "Dooly's, babe."

"Let me speak to Juarez. Right now."

"No Juarez here."

"Tell him it's Gambol."

"He's still gone."

"Don't mess around."

"I told you—he's gone."

"Where is he at?"

"I told you. He went north."

Luntz waited for a thought.

The woman said, "Who is this?"

He thumbed the disconnect and drove for several seconds holding the phone out the window, then let it drop.

Anita sat with her hands folded around the empty bottle.

The morning seemed lit by a blowtorch. The edges of his sight shimmered. "Dear Jesus, give me music." He had to spin the knob several times to get the band to move even half an inch. No music. News of this and that, a local murder.

"Did you hear that?"

Anita reached for the dial, and Luntz stopped her fingers and squeezed until she made a small sound.

"Desilvera. That's your name."

He crushed her fingers. She didn't resist.

He let her go. "That's Hank. Henry Desilvera. That's your husband."

She looked straight ahead. "Not anymore."

PART FOUR

PART FOUR

PART FOUR

JIMMY steered the pickup left-handed, his right arm crossing his chest and the right hand dangling out the window. "Did you kill him?"

Anita lifted the bottle from her lap and made sure it was perfectly empty. She wondered how Jimmy had hurt his hand.

"Did you kill your old man?" Now his right hand hopped back and forth between the gearshift and the radio knobs. "It said so on *this* radio, right *here*. Henry Desilvera. Shot to death in his home."

"God rest his soul." She closed her eyes and curled her toes around the barrel of the shotgun at her bare feet.

"I don't know what to say."

"Why don't you say 'Wow'?"

He found something and turned it up, a trio of women singing—

Tubular and tasty
Wanazee, Wanazee
Tubular and tasty

—and Jimmy said, "What?" and Anita said, "Wanazee," because it sounded magical, and Jimmy spun the knob— "Goddamn hillbilly mugwump *shit.*"

Jimmy pulled the truck over and nearly ran down a fence post and braked hard and killed the engine. In the pasture before them stood horses switching their tails, lifting their heads up and down. Jimmy said, "Let me see your gun."

"I'm not showing anybody my gun."

"I want to see if it's been fired."

"How would you know if it's been fired?"

"Let's have it." He took the revolver from her purse and shoved it under his seat. "Where are your shoes?" He gripped her knee with one hand and took the shotgun from under her feet with the other and dropped the weapon behind his seatback. "No more guns." He stuck his fingers in the pocket of his floppy shirt and came up empty and felt around the dash and got his cigarette pack, which was flat. He balled it up and threw it at the windshield in front of him and turned the key and floored the pedal, and this time he hit the fence post.

Anita stayed quiet and let him think, if that's what he was doing. He looked across the quiet farmland in front of them as if he might climb the fence and walk out into the fields and lose himself.

"I don't know what the setup is," he said. "But I know you set me up."

He reversed and got on the road and floored it again.

They sailed into Madrona, where the demands of sparse traffic seemed to help him focus. He shut up and drove halfway through town without a destination before pulling into the Alaska Burger's parking lot. He turned off the engine and gazed at the polar bear holding up a gigantic bun at the curbside.

Anita said, "I want my gun."

"No more guns."

"I'll need it when we talk to the judge."

"You set me up."

"I brought you in. You're just right. The judge has been in court. He's seen bad people."

"I'm not a thug."

"You don't know what you are. He'll know. And he's a sick old man. He's just a sack of cancer."

"Wow. You're meaner than I thought. And deeper down."

"My people are of the earth. We know who the devils are. But we love the devil. We love the devil."

He stared hard at her. Something moved in her belly like a child, and the child was Jimmy. She shut her ears to its crying, and she could feel him drawing strength from her blood. Jimmy dropped his gaze. He turned and put both hands on the wheel. He raised the left one to consult his smashed wristwatch. "How long till dark?"

"I don't know."

"We should go after dark. Does this judge have his own computer?"

"Maybe. I guess so."

"What about somebody taking care of him? Are there other people in the house?"

"I don't know."

"Then we'll scope the place right now. You know where he lives, right?"

"Yes."

"Fine. I said we had ten percent of a plan. It's more like two percent. I gotta get some smokes."

While Jimmy was gone she shut her eyes and dozed, until he ruined the moment by jerking open his door and blowing tobacco smoke and saying, "Red alert. I just saw Juarez. Or his Caddy. Or it was Gambol's Caddy. Those fuckers have identical cars." He slammed the door, it didn't catch, he slammed it again and got the truck going, looking everywhere at once like a juggler watching airborne objects. "Yeah, Gambol went and got his Caddy. Or it's Juarez. They're like high school chicks—twin Cadillacs." He drove fast, watching only the rearview mirror. "They weren't following us. They don't know this truck. Except Gambol saw it last night. But I mean—a million pickups. Unless Sally told them. Fucking Sally. Fuck. We get this done and get the fuck out. Get the fuck out and . . ." Anita sat with her eyes closed, humming "Wanazee, wanazee," and feeling the sensations of a cliff diver in a night sky while Jimmy tore through the streets and never stopped his mouth.

•

Gambol sat at the table in the breakfast nook, close to the window. Half an hour ago he'd claimed he wasn't hungry, but now that his breakfast was cold, he wanted it.

Mary put both their plates in the microwave and said, "Zapped steaks and eggs—not real good." She held up the Mumm's and tapped it with a fingernail. "What about this champagne?"

"None for me."

They heard a car outside, and Gambol watched through the window until it had passed.

Mary said, "Is the Tall Man really with him?"

"I said he was." Mary shuddered, and he added, "He's not so bad."

"How long till he comes?"

"Once you're on the Five," he said, "it's a straight shot up."

"Look good, okay? Walk tall. I want him to pay me off for resurrecting your leg. Twenty grand. This time I'll get to Montana."

"This time?"

"I've done stuff for him before. He helped me with my last big move."

"From where?"

"From here."

"You're still here."

"I didn't think big enough. I made some money, but only enough for a car."

"What did you do for him?"

"Sold him a gross of Dilaudid."

"I remember. That was you?"

"I mean a solid gross. I snatched it three days before my discharge. He made a bundle, huh?"

"Yeah."

"I didn't. I made a bunch, but less than a bundle. Was it over a hundred thousand?"

"I don't count his winnings."

"He paid me fifteen."

"You could've gotten more."

"From who? You think I know a lot of crooks?"

Gambol put his fingers on the windowsill. Another car out in the street. Mary said, "Is Juarez big in the drug trade?"

"No."

"But not entirely no. Sometimes yes."

"No, he's just—if there's a nickel to be made, he's usually the one who makes it. He's quick like that."

The microwave rang. No reaction from Gambol. By the

way he fixed his attention out the window, Mary figured she'd better go get a longer robe on.

When she came out of the bedroom, Gambol was bent over his plate, and Juarez sat across the table, watching him eat.

"This is torture," Juarez said. He looked plumper these days and pouchy around the eyes, and he seemed excited, sitting with his ankle on his knee, leaning forward, patting his fingers on the toe of his boot. He still wore those little ankle-high fruit-boots and also, this morning, a box-cut silk shirt like spun platinum with faint designs along the buttons. "I haven't had one bite since yesterday." The hem of his shirt had slipped upward over the butt of a small automatic in a clip-on holster.

Mary popped the champagne and said, "In honor of—fuck, you name it," and the cork shot out of the kitchen and landed God knows where.

She didn't go after it because the Tall Man lay on the living room couch with his shoes on the fabric and his hat over his face.

"I'm not celebrating yet. I'm hungry." Juarez pointed to the steak on the plate before him. "What about this one?"

Gambol said, "That's hers."

"Then after you eat," Juarez said, "you can watch me. We'll drive around. We'll find some breakfast. Especially we'll drive around, because I think we saw our friend—Mr. Jimmy. Ten minutes ago."

Gambol said, "Yeah?"

"A blue pickup? Ford? Real beater? But we couldn't see the license."

"The license?"

"Our other friend, he got in touch and gave me some numbers. Missy Sally."

Gambol said, "Oh."

"Yeah, Sally's still dirtying up our planet. So, you know, that other party you mentioned, the unknown person that you ran into—it's a collateral thing. Bad luck came in on a wind."

Gambol finished his steak and sopped the eggs with his toast while Juarez observed and Mary drank Mumm's from the bottle. Gambol pointed with his fork. "Your steak's getting cold."

"Go ahead," Mary told him.

Gambol exchanged his plate with hers, and Juarez sighed and said, "Mr. Gambol is a talented person. I'm glad we're associated. Proud." He turned his chair a bit and looked Mary up and down. "The Army didn't turn you into a dyke."

"Don't ask, don't tell." She took a slug of champagne.

"You put on a little weight?"

The bubbles jammed her sinuses, and she choked and whispered, "Don't ask, don't tell."

"You look good." Juarez got up and went to the living room and spoke to the Tall Man and came back holding a bulging letter-sized envelope. "Gambol also looks good. You fixed him. Look at that appetite." Even in his boots, Juarez was a bit shorter than Mary in heels. He bowed slightly, envelope extended.

She pried open the fold and thumbed through the packets. Ten of them, each wrapper marked $2000. "Paid in full."

Juarez took her hand, but he didn't shake it. He just held it. To Gambol he said, "Don't say thanks."

"I didn't."

"I know. All right, Mary. We're done here. T-Man and I need a good breakfast. Can you recommend a place where we could also talk business?"

The Tall Man came into the kitchen now. He stood under the ceiling light with his hat tipped forward and his face in a shadow and a hooked pinky traveling toward one of his nostrils, if he had nostrils.

Juarez said, "Mary?"

She turned and stood looking down into the sink.

"Where do we go for breakfast?"

"The mall. Downtown. Across from the mall."

"Is there really a downtown?"

Jesus Christ, she wanted to shout, get him out of my house.

•

Loose items scraped across the floorboard as Luntz took the first possible turn off the highway at the greatest possible speed. He tried to speak in a conversational tone. "Are they turning around?"

Anita righted herself and looked behind. "No. I mean yes. Now they are."

"It's them. They know the truck."

Anita grabbed his arm for stability as he took the next road coming. "I don't see them now."

"That Caddy will eat this thing." They passed between open pastures, completely exposed. "Watch behind. Hang on."

"Not this one." With her left hand she stopped the wheel. "Go two more."

He checked his mirror. "There they are. It doesn't matter where we turn."

"Next one. Next one. This one."

"Stay off my gearshift."

The pastureland ended. They sped through a tract of homes. He zigzagged among the blocks, feeling safer with walls around him. He didn't see the Caddy. But it had to be near.

"Go faster."

Luntz went slower. "We have to ditch this truck." He watched for any kind of alley, an open garage door, any semi-enclosed space.

Anita leaned hard against him and grabbed and forced the wheel, saying, "Left, left, left," and would have steered them onto somebody's porch if he hadn't braked hard and cut the corner across a lawn and onto a perpendicular street.

"Jesus. Where are they?"

"No. No. See the house up there? We can go in."

"Here?"

"That one, that one." She was digging for something in her purse. "Not the driveway. Don't block the car. Park beside the house." She was opening her door as he floored it and whipped around a large sedan in the driveway and fishtailed around the side of the house and scraped against the neighboring fence and stopped, trapping his own door shut. He took hold of the shotgun and scrambled to follow her out the passenger door, hesitated two seconds, and lay across the seat and felt for Anita's revolver on the floorboards.

She was already at the front door. He followed, concealing, he hoped, the shotgun between his arm and his ribs, its muzzle in his hand and the pistol grip in his armpit, meanwhile sticking the revolver in his waist and untucking his shirt to cover it. He joined her on the porch.

She held a set of keys. She was reading a red notice fixed to the door, its message printed in black capital letters. Across the door a stretch of yellow flagging—CRIME SCENE DO NOT CROSS CRIME SCENE DO NOT CROSS.

She tore away the yellow flagging, and Luntz said, "Hey."

She unlocked the door and threw it wide and strode inside.

Luntz took two steps into the interior and was stopped by the silence it held—a sunken living room with a thick cream carpet and a wooden bar, a hallway beyond it prohibited by the same yellow flagging, and something in the hallway, maybe a lamp or a sculpture, shrouded with a black plastic bag.

He heard Anita in the kitchen banging cabinets open and closed and saying, "Fucker. Fucker. Fucker."

Luntz stepped down into the living room and crossed the carpet and broke the yellow banner and traveled the hallway to the open door at its end. A king-sized bed, mussed bedclothes, a wine-red hardwood floor, not much blood on it—maybe half a cup of coagulated jelly around the left armpit of a white outline with upflung arms and very short legs. For some seconds, Luntz couldn't take his eyes from it. The chalk-person had no legs below the knees.

Outside the bedroom lay a garden. Large leaves and large dark blossoms nodded at the window. Luntz wiped his mouth with a fist and felt his lips moving. He edged sideways out the door, and halfway down the hall he turned and hurried to the kitchen.

Anita stood at the counter, unscrewing the lid of a cookie jar. "Come on." Car keys.

"Get me out of here," he said. She turned the deadbolt, and he followed her out the kitchen door, saying, "This is destroying my nerves." She led him into the garden and around the side and then to the sedan out front. "I gotta say, you have a calm disposition." They got in the car, and she was out of there fast but quiet, not quite peeling rubber. "Yeah. A calm exterior." They were topping seventy-five on a suburban street. "You're efficient. That's what it is." He swiped his forearm across his sweaty face. Under his shirt the perspiration poured over his ribs. "Holy Toledo!" he said. "Don't you ever get nervous?"

•

Jimmy laid the shotgun between them on the seat. Anita covered it with her purse, as much of it as she could, and lowered the windows for air while Jimmy lit up and blew his smoke all over the place. "Damn," Jimmy said, "this is a Jaguar. This is yours?"

"Nothing's mine."

"This is real wood, isn't it?" He was touching things.

Suddenly they were downtown, and she felt stupid. "I went the wrong way. Everybody in town knows this Jag."

"Find a parking garage."

"It's a hundred miles to a parking garage."

The Madrona Mall consisted of the Rex Theater and the Osco Drug and half a dozen other storefronts, a couple of them empty, their plate glass faced with plywood. She drove behind the Rex and stopped in the alley behind an orange backhoe and a pile of asphalt rubble.

Jimmy said, "Now what? How long till it's dark?"

"Quit asking. I'm not the sun."

He lifted his shirttail. "This weapon has to go."

"It's mine."

"It's trash. There's a body on it. All it is now," he said, "is evidence." He shoved her revolver under his seat.

She leaned across him and felt for it, but he kicked it back farther out of reach.

"I want my gun."

Jimmy sat up and got quite still and said, "When you jerked the trigger, he fell straight back. He was on his knees."

The ashtray stank. She closed it.

"Yeah," he said, "on his knees." He settled back and shut his eyes.

She turned off the ignition and let her thoughts go away. Her head jerked up—she'd nodded off. Jimmy sat with his head back, his eyelids down, breathing loudly through his open mouth.

She felt the child moving inside her again, the child who was Jimmy. She shut it away, but its cries broke through.

"Jimmy. Jimmy."

"What?"

"We're two blocks from the cop shop. Less than two."

He rubbed his eyes and his face with both hands and lit a cigarette. "Two what?"

"Blocks. The police station. If you keep heading down the street we were on—there's a white globe out front."

"Well, Anita . . . I'm sure this is all true."

"What have you done that's so bad? They'll protect you."

"Who—the cops?"

"They'll keep you alive, at least."

"The cops? You want me to shit on this whole thing and go to the cops?"

"Are they any more horrible than these other people?"

"Jesus Christ—the cops? Yes. There's no comparison."

He smoked, looking at his cigarette.

She closed her eyes and slept.

•

To Gambol's thinking, the neighborhood seemed exactly like the one around Mary's place, a suburban tract staring at a mountain wilderness. He swept his gaze into wide living-room windows as Juarez took the Cadillac slowly along.

Plenty of pickup trucks. Some of them blue. None of them Fords.

The Tall Man had the rear seat to himself. He shifted to its middle, and Juarez reached up and adjusted the mirror to eliminate him from the view.

Gambol heard the Tall Man's throat work. Maybe he was drinking a drink. His hand appeared on the back of Juarez's seat. You found yourself looking mostly at his hands.

The Tall Man said, "Up ahead."

"Oh, my, too bad." Juarez took a left, following the general direction of two parallel gouges cutting the corner of a lawn. "Somebody's driving reckless."

At the next street, Juarez turned left once more and accelerated to the middle of the block. Gambol put his hand on the dash as he braked before a house whose front door lay wide open. To the side, between the house and the fence, sat the blue Ford.

Gambol shifted his cane and unlatched his door, and Juarez said, "Spare yourself. T-Man, will you go and poke your head in?"

The Tall Man stood about five feet, eight inches. They watched him stride across the lawn. He wore a brown business suit and a 1950s fedora hat tipped far forward and yellow old-man shoes, but he moved like a man of about middle age.

Juarez laid his right arm across the seatback, and Gambol moved his own arm away and took the head of his cane and repositioned it pointlessly.

"This is a crime scene," Juarez said.

Gambol noticed the bright streamer curled on the porch, a tattered end of it lifting and collapsing, readjusted by the breeze.

Juarez said, "What do you think?"

"They changed rides."

"The garage is right there," Juarez said. "Stupid, stupid. They should've stashed the truck. What do you think they took? I mean the car."

"Do I look psychic?"

"This is a nice neighborhood. They took a nice car."

The Tall Man returned and opened the Caddy's rear

door. "Nobody home." He got in and shut the door and settled himself and said, "That's a crime scene in there."

"Keep alert." Juarez put it in gear. "We'll take a zigzag route. Watch out for a nice car driving stupid."

The Tall Man said, "Do we have a destination?"

"Breakfast. Downtown."

●

Jimmy Luntz woke with a spasm. He'd fallen asleep at the wheel. But there was no wheel. He was a passenger. As the day reassembled itself around him he wondered if something, maybe the backhoe in front of them, had fallen from the sky onto this beautiful Jaguar. But it appeared they'd been struck from behind.

Anita said, "Jimmy."

Juarez stood beside Luntz's window, signaling that it should be lowered.

Gambol flanked Anita's window. As she tried to open her door, he slammed it shut. She turned the key in the ignition, but there was no place to go.

Luntz moved his hand along the armrest, thinking fast but producing no thoughts, and his window came down.

Juarez stooped to put his face in Luntz's. "We had a little crash, and I'm sorry. But everything's fine. We'll take you exactly where you're going."

●

Gambol opened the woman's door. She was looking at the shotgun beside her on the seat.

He watched her right hand. She hesitated, then placed her hand on the steering wheel and her foot on the pavement and got out of the car. Her feet were bare.

Luntz addressed Juarez: "Is that your Caddy, or Gambol's?"

"This one's mine," Juarez said, crossing around behind the Caddy to open the back door. "Luntz first." Luntz got in the car and Juarez said, "Our lady in back also." The woman obeyed.

The Tall Man sat at the wheel. By the tilt of his hat Gambol guessed he was studying the woman in his review mirror.

Gambol slapped at Luntz's window until the Tall Man lowered it. He rapped on the trunk lid with his cane until he heard its lock unlatch. He hung his cane on the sill and leaned down and put a forefinger hard against Luntz's left eyeball. "I want your shirt." Luntz worked at the buttons, and Gambol took his finger away and hauled the shirt from around Luntz and went to the Jaguar and wrapped the shotgun in it and put the bundle in the Caddy's trunk.

Juarez had his hands on the Caddy's windowsill on the woman's side. He lowered himself to peer within. "Look at those dirty little feet."

Gambol returned to Luntz's window and extended the flat of his palm under Luntz's nose. "My wallet." Luntz shifted in his seat and dug at his pants and produced the wallet. Gambol gave him two across the face with it, back and forth, and then put it in his pocket without examination. Luntz sat there with his eyes watering, shirtless, chicken-chested. "Luntz. A twelve-gauge is not a magic wand. You don't wave it around and people just explode."

Luntz's woman laughed.

Gambol told her, "I don't like you."

"That's all right," Juarez said, reaching toward her lap to touch her hand, which was a fist, "everybody else in the world is very fond of her. And she's going to give you the keys to the Jaguar, right, Mr. G.? And we'll follow you back to Mary's place. And you'll call Mary and tell her not to be home, and leave the garage door open."

•

Luntz squeezed Anita's knee twice, signaling something, he didn't know what, while Juarez got into the back seat on Anita's other side and looked her up and down and said, "Boy."

The Tall Man drove, following the Jag along the avenues. Juarez watched Anita's face as much as the view ahead. Anita sat still. Juarez said, "She's slightly beyond you, Luntz. Another class of person."

Luntz said, "I know."

"What's her name?"

Luntz said, "Anita."

"What's her last name?"

"Desilvera."

They were on the highway for five minutes before turning into another of Madrona's subdivisions. The Tall Man drove slowly, his arm out the window and his hand urging the Jaguar to continue down the block. "The garage is still closed." At the end of the block the Tall Man stopped the car behind the Jag and put it in park.

Luntz said, "Fucking Sally. Sally the snitch." He hunched his bare shoulders and wrapped himself in his arms. "I should've beaten him to death with the shovel. Spade. The spade."

The Tall Man raised the windows and turned on the climate control.

Juarez said, "Anita."

"Yes."

"Your eyes are a little bit tightened up, and I'd like it better if you can relax."

"Okay."

"Nothing's going to happen to you. This isn't your day for that."

Anita was staring at the back of the Tall Man's hat. Luntz squeezed her thigh hard, but she didn't blink. She said, "Okay."

The Tall Man put the car in gear, saying, "There she goes," and executed a high-velocity U-turn and drove to the middle of the block and into a garage and parked beside the Jaguar.

Gambol got out of the Jag and hit a wall switch, and the

garage door descended. When its rumbling ceased, Gambol approached, shifted his cane to his left hand, and pulled open Luntz's door.

Juarez said, "Anita. We're going inside here. You want to come inside with us?"

"No."

Juarez said, "Luntz is coming. Right, Luntz?" as Gambol took hold of Luntz's arm.

Juarez opened his door and said to the Tall Man, "Get her inside."

•

The Tall Man delayed. The others had moved into the house, but the collision point of certain energies remained here, in the car, with this woman.

"These others," he told her, "don't know what they are."

He turned the key to provide power to the windows and lowered them all and said, "I'll smoke."

He twisted toward her in his seat. For a few seconds he paused, letting the scent of the others leave the interior. He said, "You're beautiful."

"Thank you."

He raised his face as his lighter flamed so that its glow illuminated him under the hat brim. "It's a burden, isn't it?"

"Yes."

He held the flame for many seconds. She didn't look away. He'd been quite sure she wouldn't.

"These others," he told her once more, "don't know what they are." He trusted she'd understood him the first time, but it merited repeating.

"Will they let Jimmy live?"

"No."

"Oh," she said.

"What about you? Do you smoke?"

She shook her head.

"I'm going in. Will you come along?"

"Okay."

•

"Sit." Juarez took Anita's arm gently, but she couldn't shake him off. "You don't like me touching you," he said. He moved the ottoman aside for her, and she sat on the couch. He came in close. "It's not about you watching. You understand?"

"No."

"It's about him," Juarez said, "watching you watching."

Jimmy occupied a dining chair set in the middle of a spread of silvery plastic tarp. He wasn't watching her.

The person called Tall Man set a similar chair in the corner across the living room. He sat down and turned on the lamp on the sideboard so that he occupied a shadow.

Gambol snapped his fingers in her face. "Give me your belt."

Anita took her belt off and handed it to him. He knelt

and looped Jimmy's left ankle to a chair leg and ran the belt around the chair's opposite leg, taking up the slack, and buckled it, and Anita believed he said, "It's a tourniquet— ha ha," but Anita couldn't hear, because Jimmy himself was talking.

"—and this old guy moved in like three places down from us," Jimmy was saying. "It was a trailer park. I think I was twelve. Dude told me he'd pay me twenty dollars a day to clean up his trailer before he moved in. 'Clean up my trailer, twenty bucks per day.' Gave me disinfectant and a bucket and all that shit."

"Shut up," Gambol said. He stood. He handed Juarez a box cutter and said, "There's some bungees in the garage." He went out through the kitchen.

Holding the box cutter, Juarez put his hands in the pockets of his slacks, standing with the sharp toes of his boots at the outer edge of the tarpaulin, looking at Jimmy.

"Took me four and a half eight-hour days to get it clean. There was crap everywhere. There was dirt underneath the dirt. I washed the floors like three times, and after that I had to scrape with a putty knife. I really washed that place down. Got all the clutter out of the yard, raked up all the little sticks into a pile. Then I had to dig stuff out of the dirt with my fingers, broken bits of plastic, who knows what it was. Stuff gets broken. Plastic stuff. Got all of it in the back of his pickup, had a different brand of tire on every wheel. Hosed down the little strip of asphalt in the front. Scattered seed, man, for the lawn. Took me four and half days to get it like new. Never worked that hard before or since. And at the end of this, he explained the whole thing to me carefully."

Gambol came in through the kitchen and stood by the counter with a tangle of bungee cords dangling from his hand.

"This dude—I'd say he was sixty, maybe. Drawing disability, periodic drunk, family gone, you know what I mean, just your typical solitary human wreck. And he says, 'I've got ninety dollars for you. You sure earned it, and I've got it. Or you can have this lottery ticket.' Out it comes. Yeah, big old card in the palm of his hand. 'This ticket,' he says, 'cost a dollar fifty. So if I pay you the ninety, you could find somebody to buy you sixty tickets just like it. Or you can take this one. Just this one.' Yeah. That's right. Yeah. So I took it."

Juarez said, "You think I don't know why you're telling me this?"

"I don't know. Maybe you do and maybe you don't."

Juarez ceased jiggling his hands in his pockets. "I don't have to ask if it hit."

Nothing from Jimmy.

"Fuck you. You lost."

Over in his corner, the Tall Man coughed. Or laughed.

•

It occurred to Luntz the era of Quiet Jimmy had ended. Words had worn his throat raw. "I just want you to know who you're killing."

"I didn't say I'm killing you," Juarez told him. "What's happening is I'm about to cut off your balls. If you die of it, that's your personal decision."

He dragged the ottoman to the tarp, lifting its legs a little to get it over the plastic's edge, and sat down facing Luntz, their knees nearly touching.

Gambol raised his bungees and began extricating a cord from the tangle.

"This is so depressing," Luntz said.

"Gambol, did you hear that? Luntz is getting depressed."

"I mean it. What's depressing is this two-point-five million dollars I'll never get to spend."

"Wolf tickets."

"Actually, it's not so depressing. Either way—I win."

"The fuck you do. Watching your balls get eaten isn't exactly winning. Very closely similar to losing, that's my opinion."

"Watching you fuck up a chance at millions of dollars makes it all okay," Luntz said.

"He's bullshit," Gambol said.

"Fine all around," Luntz said, unbuttoning his farmer denims. "Where's your knife and fork, asshole?" He opened his pants and pulled the elastic of his shorts under his testicles.

Juarez said, "Gambol, do you see this?"

"Yeah."

"He just got out his equipment."

"Let's eat," Gambol said.

Juarez drew his head back and regarded Luntz as if through a bad pair of glasses. "You're a poker player."

Luntz said, "Wait a minute."

Juarez leaned in close. "What just happened to your eyes?"

"I made a mistake. It's two-point-three. Not two-point-five. Two-point-three."

Juarez stared very carefully into Luntz's eyes. "I gotta admit," he said . . . but it took him a long minute to admit anything . . . "your pupils are normal."

"Two-point-three million dollars. That's what it's going to cost you to—you know. Your famous act."

"I have to get your face away from me." Juarez rose and went to the kitchen and sat at the table by the window. Gambol and the Tall Man stayed quiet, and Luntz, so as not to look at Anita, closed his eyes and sat holding perhaps for the last time his manhood in one hand.

After two minutes Juarez stood, turned, and resumed the ottoman facing Luntz. "Do you know why you're not dead?"

Luntz said nothing, because he didn't know the answer.

"Because you called me 'asshole.' That was the touch. That was the touch right there."

As Luntz made a slight motion, Juarez said, "But don't put your balls away yet. Somebody has to draw me a map to the treasure."

Luntz looked at Anita.

Her eyes raced around the room as if a mob were tearing her clothes off. "I still want my half."

•

Mary looked smart today—gray skirt, spiked heels, tight white blouse. Not, Gambol hoped, for the benefit of Juarez. You can't blame a woman for looking good.

She asked for a cell phone with a restricted ID. Juarez handed her his.

She signaled for silence, though the others were silent already—Gambol himself, Juarez standing over Luntz, Luntz's woman shrunken into the couch, the Tall Man against the wall.

She sat on the ottoman, put a cigarette in her lips, set her purse aside, and crossed her legs. She punched the buttons while holding her lighter in her hand.

"This is Louise. I'm the sub today . . . No, Kilene can't make it. I just thought I'd check in with you. How's he doing? . . . Any special instructions? They said he doesn't need to be lifted—is that right?" She lit her cigarette and smoked awhile. "Okay, dumb question—when am I supposed to be there? . . . Damn"—she leaned backward to see the kitchen's wall clock—"I'll be about fifteen minutes late. You go ahead and leave—he can go fifteen minutes on his own, right?" She took the phone to the kitchen counter.

"Listen, I want to check in with the agency, but I'm in the car—have you got the number handy? And what's the patient's full name?"

She made a note on a pad on the counter and came back to the ottoman, punching buttons.

"This is Eloise Tanneau. I'm Judge Tanneau's niece. I'm looking after him tonight, so can we skip the night nurse? And he may be coming home with me a few days . . . Probably next Wednesday. I'll call first thing tomorrow and let you know for sure."

She closed the phone and put out her cigarette and crossed her legs and clasped both hands around her knee, leaning forward. "Phew!"

Juarez said, "I should've never divorced you."

"Yeah? I divorced you."

Gambol watched all this.

Juarez went into a corner with the Tall Man and spoke to him, looking only at the Tall Man's yellow shoes. Gambol heard him say, "Jag-you-are."

He came back to Gambol and said, "I want the Jag," and Gambol turned over the keys.

Juarez pointed to the Tall Man, pointed to Luntz's woman. "Take him. Take her. Mary goes to the movies." He lifted the sharp toe of his boot and rested it on the chair between Luntz's legs. "Leave this customer with me."

Mary said, "I just saw the fucking movie. Twice."

Juarez said, "Stay away for one hour. Keep your phone on."

Mary touched the back of Gambol's hand with all four fingers. "See you later."

Juarez observed the gesture. "See," Juarez said angrily, "this is what I like about people. People surprise you."

●

Luntz counted himself still in the game—his pants still open, but his balls back inside his shorts. But alone with Juarez, and Juarez holding an automatic pistol.

"Gambol won't like it if you're the one who smokes me."

"I'll like it."

"I'm just saying—you know. Friends like to do things together."

"I want his Cadillac. It isn't your property. Give me the keys."

"The keys are in it. Sort of. More like sitting on the roof of it."

"Where's it parked?"

"About three miles off the main highway. Then way up there. Up the Feather River."

"You piece of shit. Let's go."

"Now?"

Juarez sighed.

"Unbuckle my leg."

"Unbuckle your own leg."

Luntz managed the belt, but he didn't feel capable of standing. "What are we doing?"

"We'll drive there, and we'll get his car."

"And then what?"

"Then I'll present it to him. When he gets back from what he's doing."

"And your car's going to be—where? Where his car is now?"

"Yeah."

"I don't understand."

"That's because you exist," Juarez said, "at the level of a lizard. Gambol will understand the gesture."

They stood side by side as the door thundered and the last of the day's light filled the garage. Juarez nudged him into the passenger's side with the point of his gun. "Ladies first." He lifted his shirt and holstered the pistol. "Remember who has the power."

While Juarez moved to the driver's side and opened the door, Luntz felt around beneath the seat. Juarez got in, saying, "This is a test drive. I'm considering a Jag-you-are." As he reached his hand toward the ignition, Luntz put Anita's gun to his neck.

•

The Tall Man removed his hat and set it on the dashboard and turned almost fully toward Anita in the back seat. He counted four seconds before she looked away. He said, "What? I thought you said something," because he wanted her to.

"Excuse me?"

"What sort of car does this judge drive?"

"It's in the garage."

"I realize. But what kind is it?"

"A Cadillac."

"Like this one."

"But it's black."

The house belonged in New England—stone walls and dark vines of ivy, a big entry with stained glass either side of the door. Gambol had been standing at the door a long time.

"This man is very slow answering. You said he's in a wheelchair, correct?"

"I didn't say that."

"No. You're right. Mary said it."

They had the Cadillac running and the windows closed for the air conditioner, but the sound from the house was audible to them as Gambol broke a pane of leaded glass with the butt of his revolver. They watched his shoulders rock slightly as he scoured the jagged edges of the pane with the gun's barrel, and then he turned sideways and slipped his arm up to its elbow into the interior.

Anita said, "What?"

"I said, are you worried about Luntz?"

"Yes."

"And you're sure this man has a computer on the premises?"

"What? Yes. I mean, I think so."

"Luntz is dead by now."

"Oh."

He breathed the syllable in. He tasted heartbreak. "His last moments were impressive. Do you think he kept his balls?"

"Oh . . . his balls?"

He inhaled deeply. The cell phone hummed twice in his hand. He checked the ID. "That's Gambol." He shut off the car's engine. He replaced his hat and pulled the brim down as far as visibility permitted and headed for the house without looking to see if she followed.

Inside, he left the front door open behind him and waited for her. By the front door, a hat-tree. On the hat-tree a dark suit coat on a hanger. He ran a finger down its empty sleeve. Italian silk. Gambol stood in the kitchen mistreating the jacket's owner. Above them and around them, tinted skylights and green potted plants gave the kitchen and dining areas a cool, pleasant feeling.

Even in his wheelchair the man gave an impression of height, some of it established by his coiffure—brilliant, silver-white, layered like a toupee, which plainly it wasn't, as Gambol had his fingers tangled in it, pulling the man's head backward in his wheelchair to prevent him fixing the buttons of his shirt. When the man let his hands down, Gambol let go of his hair.

"I found him in the bathroom."

Except for the omission of his suitcoat, the man had dressed for business, his slacks perfectly creased, shoes a brilliant black on the wheelchair's metal footpads, but beneath the knot of his crimson tie his shirt was unbuttoned and its tails untucked, and a colostomy bag jutted from under his left armpit.

The door slammed behind the Tall Man, and Anita strode past him toward the kitchen. In her lumberjack costume, in her bare feet, still this female knew how to walk— head up, shoulders back—away from a flaming wreck. She bore down on the man, saying, "I'm guilty, Judge."

The judge possessed a histrionic flair. At the sight of Anita his chin went up, and his eyes grew shiny.

"I killed Hank." Now Anita stood before the wheelchair. With both her hands she grasped the bag under his armpit and jerked it free and struck him across the face with it, putting half a pirouette behind the blow, and Gambol leapt aside as feces erupted down the man's neck and chest and behind his back, so that he was wearing it and sitting in it.

The judge raised his hand to wipe at his face but seemed to think better of it. He tilted his head, probably to direct the flow, and breathed through his open mouth.

Gambol said something too softly to be heard, and the Tall Man said, "Shut up. We're out of our depth."

•

Juarez drove right-handed, the heel of his left hand stanching the flow of blood from his forehead. "I love getting pistol-whipped. It means I'm dealing with a *puto*. He can't pull the trigger."

"Get to the highway." Luntz switched the gun from his right hand to his left, keeping the weapon pressed against Juarez's kidney, and sat back in a posture he believed more natural-looking for a passenger and added, "Shut up."

"I wasn't talking."

"You were before."

"Where to?"

"Shut up."

"Where are we going, Luntz?"

"Turn left up here. Left. What do you smoke?" As they accelerated onto the highway, he reached into Juarez's shirt pocket. "Lites. Crap."

"No, they're good. Really."

"Low-tar. Silk shirt. Hey. Got any money?"

"Money?" Juarez lowered his window, and the hot breeze thudded around their heads.

"Give it here."

Leaning forward and squirming in his seat, Juarez got his money clip from the pocket of his slacks and threw it out the window.

"You fucking *fuck*." Luntz put the muzzle under Juarez's jaw and pressed until Juarez craned his neck and grimaced. At the sight of oncoming cars, Luntz lowered it to the area of Juarez's ribs.

Juarez wiped the blood out of his eye and then onto

the seat, between his legs. "What's your next move? Go to this judge's house and waste everybody? Run off with the girl over your shoulder?"

Luntz ignored him and made use of the Jag's cigarette lighter.

"What a hero. You never even thought about Anita. You don't deserve her."

"What's the address?"

"I don't know, Luntz. Don't you know?" A sports convertible pulled around on their left. Juarez said, "Look—those girls are laughing at your chest."

"Let them pass. Asshole."

Juarez accelerated gently, keeping abreast of the convertible. "You're an embarrassment. If Anita's your woman, then save her."

"She's not my woman," Luntz said. "And nobody can save her."

Juarez clenched the wheel, working his thumbs. "You're an embarrassment from the beginning." He turned his face toward Luntz. He was red-eyed, almost tearful. "When you pull a gun, you know what's the next thing to do? *Shoot* the gun. *Shoot* somebody." The Jaguar lurched into passing gear.

"Slow down, Juarez."

"Let's put on a show."

"Slow down."

Juarez stomped and released the accelerator rhythmically and rocked the engine in and out of passing gear. "See up there, the overpass?"

"I'm serious, Juarez."

"What I'm going to do, I'm going to drive into the abutment."

Luntz stuck the gun barrel in Juarez's ear and was pressed back in his seat. The engine's noise rose steadily.

"Fuck you, Luntz. Put the gun down, or I swear to fuck." Juarez levitated in his seat as he locked his leg, holding the pedal to the floor. "We'll break one-twenty." He was shouting above the engine's noise. "I die, you die. Come on, I been waiting for a reason to crash this piece-of-shit Jag. I think I'll get a Lexus."

Thinking, What a good line, how cool is this guy Juarez, Luntz blew his head off. Juarez's window collapsed into rice grains while a two-inch-wide fissure opened above his ear. Luntz clutched the wheel with one hand and then with both hands, and the gun fell into Juarez's lap while Luntz nearly followed it, working his left leg over the console and kicking at Juarez's pointed boot on the accelerator. He found the brake with his foot and pulled the wheel to the right, and now they traveled backward, and the view smeared itself across the windshield, and now they'd swapped ends again and were stopped diagonally on the gravel shoulder. The engine had quit. In the silence it ticked, and Luntz heard himself breathing hard and saying, "Wow. I think I just shot you."

"We wrap a towel around here, just below the knee," Gambol explained to the judge, "and we go berzerk with a tire iron. What the fuck is this?"

"My catheter bag."

"Jesus," Gambol said.

"Make him beg," Anita said.

"I'm seventy-six years of age. Do you understand? My bones won't heal."

The Tall Man suspected the judge's resistance had more to do with his shock at bad manners than with any worldly desire to keep his money. The man was very ill, with a jaundiced tint to his faded suntan and a papery, tentative quality to his flesh, to say nothing of his colostomy bag—and the catheter bag too, peeking from the cuff of his slacks.

"Don't worry," Gambol told the judge, "you'll probably talk before the bone splits."

"I'll talk now," the judge said. "It won't help you, but I'm at your mercy."

"That's how it works," Gambol said.

"No. No," Anita said. "He's the father of lies."

"What the fuck," Gambol asked her, "is your name?"

"Anita."

"Shut up, Anita." With the corner of a dish towel, Gambol wiped shit from the judge's cheek. "The Tall Man's got some questions."

The judge took the dish towel in his fingers and rubbed

his neck with it. "I'm sure I know what you want." He folded the cloth around the soiled portion and rubbed at his chin.

"You've hidden some funds," the Tall Man said. "We want account numbers, passwords, all of that."

"Look under the kitchen trash."

Gambol hauled a white plastic bucket from under the sink and set it by the wheelchair. "Go through your own trash."

"Under the bag. The steps are listed in order."

Gambol hoisted the trash bag and felt around beneath it and threw a notebook on the counter, beside the Tall Man's elbow.

"Something important now." The judge took a long breath. "I've given you what I can, but it's only half of what you want. There's an eight-digit password. When we chose it, I typed in four digits, and my partner typed in four. You understand? You've got half the password. My partner had the other half."

"Get him here."

"There I can't oblige you either." The judge turned his eyes on Anita. "My partner's been killed."

Anita stood straight and silent. Gambol said, "Get her purse."

"There's nothing in my purse." As if probing for the limit of her physical freedom, Anita moved aside the trash bag and went to the kitchen sink and started the water and splashed her hands and face. The Tall Man watched for some explosive move. He believed in her.

She raised her flannel shirttails and wiped her face and said, "There's nothing written down. But as long as I get my half, we're fine."

"That," Gambol said, "is not how it works."

She stepped quickly toward the end of the kitchen and the door to the yard. Gambol came after just as quickly but stumbled on the trash bag and slipped on wet floor tiles and went down on one knee, and the Tall Man felt something flare in his own chest and might even, he believed, have said, "Go!" At the door she clutched the knob and worked at the chain lock. Gambol caught the waist of her pants and pulled her backward as he stood up. He grasped her left wrist and dragged her through the kitchen toward the hallway, twisting her arm behind her and shoving his fist in her mouth so one could hardly hear the noise she made when her shoulder dislocated. Convulsively she puked on his hand, and he took it away and flung the liquid at the floor, saying, "That's it—no mercy," and she said, "Good."

•

The judge's study was dark. As the Tall Man pressed the keys and woke the computer, the screen lit the backs of his hands at the keyboard.

He paused to button his suit jacket and place his hands over his lap and listen to the sounds from the neighboring room.

When the sounds had stopped, the Tall Man moved his fingers over the keys and opened communications with the bank.

The judge said, "Excuse me. I don't like to disturb you. But I have a question."

"Yes?"

"This situation. Is it going to be terminal? In your opinion."

"For Anita?"

"For anyone. For me."

There came a thump, just one. The Tall Man raised a finger for silence. No more sounds came. His fingers returned to the keyboard.

When he heard the door to the other room open and close, he raised his face to the wall before him. "In here."

Gambol entered the study and shut the door, holding in his hand a small piece of paper. "Try this." A yellow Post-it note.

"The other hand."

Gambol transferred it to his bloody hand, and the Tall Man accepted it and fixed the paper next to the notebook open at his elbow.

"I don't push buttons on machines," Gambol told the judge. "Just people. So I hope you know what happens if this password's bullshit."

"Quiet." The Tall Man pushed his chair back and stood up.

He went down the short hallway and stood for a moment outside the door. He put his hand on the doorknob and let it stay there. She was still making small sounds.

When Gambol coughed in the next room and the Tall Man felt he might be about to call out, he let go of the doorknob and let go of it all and returned to the judge's study.

He sat before the keyboard and entered the password and waited.

"How long does this shit take?" Gambol said, making it a question for their host rather than the Tall Man.

The judge gave no indication of having heard him.

"This one's working." The Tall Man rested his chin in his hand and awaited further prompts from the machine.

"Then I guess you transfer it to the Caymans. I wonder if that's the same bank as mine," Gambol said to no one.

The Tall Man tapped the keys and waited.

"How do you get the money out?" Gambol asked the judge.

The Tall Man said, "I log in to the bank's site and then follow the prompts."

"How do you log in to the bank?"

"First," the Tall Man said, "you learn about computers."

"You got a pen?" Gambol asked the judge.

The Tall Man said, "Yes, I do." Simultaneously he felt a gun nuzzling his collar.

In the many years of their association, Gambol had addressed the Tall Man perhaps half a dozen times directly. He did so now. "Write it all down."

•

At the intersection with the highway, Gambol stopped the Caddy. He reached crosswise with his left hand and levered the gearshift into park. The Tall Man faced straight ahead.

Gambol patted the pockets of the Tall Man's jacket and took away his cell phone and his notebook and laid them on the console and nudged the Tall Man's ribs with the gun.

The Tall Man opened his door and got out. Gambol shut it for him by accelerating away.

A quarter mile along the highway, Gambol took his foot off the accelerator and laid his wrists on the wheel and worked his shoulders. The traffic was bad. The problem was on the other side, in a northbound lane, but vehicles here in the southbound lane had slowed to a walking pace. At this speed, the Tall Man might beat him to Madrona.

He checked his mirror and saw the Tall Man ambling behind him toward town in the cool of the evening, his silhouette raised up and set aside by passing headlights.

The Tall Man handled numbers, taxes, accounts. He'd set up Gambol's own offshore tax dodge. Gambol liked him.

He dropped his hand and found the button and backed his seat out to the fullest extent and eased the angle of his right leg. He got Mary on the phone and said, "What do you know about computers?"

"I know they make me sick. The last few years in the service, I had to be online every day."

"I need you to jump on a computer for me."

"Whose phone are you using? I almost didn't answer."

"Compliments of a friend."

The vehicles around him flickered in a blue and white light. As he idled the Caddy past the scene of the trouble, he nearly stopped. Accidents were none of his business, gawking just another symptom of the human disease. But he thought he recognized the car.

•

She woke in a red darkness. The sound of the river lifted her to her feet and carried her down a tunnel that branched toward light and the noise of water.

In the brilliant chamber the judge sat stripped naked, leaning sideways in his wheelchair, wetting a white flag under a faucet. The judge pronounced her sentence: "You're alive."

Give me your car keys, she said, but it didn't sound like that because her jaw must be broken.

"I called to you many times. I thought they'd killed you." He made no attempt to cover himself.

Keys.

"Did you say keys?"

Car.

"Go lie down."

She ordered her hands to his throat. Only the right one obeyed.

"It's a 1951 Coupe de Ville. I bought it secondhand the day I passed the bar. I won't let you wreck it."

She put the crook of her thumb and forefinger against his Adam's apple and felt for the arteries below either jaw.

He took her wrist in both his hands, and his eyes turned cold. "In the kitchen. On the bulletin board."

Her tendons burned where his fingernails gouged against the back of her hand. His face paled, and a faint blue light dawned beneath the skin. He lost consciousness within seconds, but still he breathed. She shifted her stance and tightened her grip on his larynx, and a wheezing began. She closed her eyes and directed all awareness into the effort of her right hand. No sight or sound reached her senses. She couldn't have said which one of them was dying.

•

With the washer's noise out in the utility room, Mary wasn't certain she'd heard a car. She hit the mute on the television and stood up as Gambol came through the front door.

He raised the end of his cane and pointed it at her and said, "Man, you look good today."

"I clean up pretty nice, huh?"

"Hey," he said, "let's take a ride."

She kicked at her pumps and slipped her feet into them and stooped to put out her cigarette. "I've got laundry in. Can I turn it off?"

"Leave it."

She looked toward the utility room where the machine chugged and gurgled. She reached for the remote and dropped it and knelt on the carpet, feeling for it under the coffee table.

"Leave it."

She stood up. "Ernest. I never saw you smile before."

"Is there fishing in Montana?"

"Every square inch." She drew her head back. "You've got nice teeth."

He dropped his cane and took her in his arms. "The Muslims lost one today."

"Yeah, baby," she said. "Nuke Mecca."

•

The right-hand tires bumped over onto the shoulder, she yanked the wheel straight, they very soon bumped over again. Did she need gas? That thought came in and went away. Was it really raining?—when the stars were shining? She found the button and lowered the window and stuck her head out for great breaths of chilly air, driving one-handed, covering her shattered eye socket with the other hand to eliminate the duplicates in her field of vision.

The big black Cadillac divided the rain. She killed the headlamps. The downpour glittered in the starshine, in the moonglow, in the lightning. Sure was raining hard. Sure was looking bad. At this rate, she'd never make it to the river.

•

Jimmy Luntz walked the road, watching his feet by starlight. Along the pavement's edge, tufts of grass sprouted from the asphalt.

He came to a crossing—a gas station and convenience store—and went inside and said, "Nice night."

The gal behind the counter said, "No shirt, no shoes, no service."

"I have shoes on."

She said, "Sorry," and seemed sincere. She looked young, and possibly pregnant, or ready for a diet.

He checked his money clip.

"Kenny's in the back," she said.

"I wasn't looking for him."

"I know. But just so you know."

"Do I look like a robber?"

"You look like something. Not a robber. Just along those lines."

"How much are those T-shirts?"

"Whatever it says."

From the bin he picked one—light blue, size large, MORE BEER—and pulled it over his head.

"That one's funny," she said.

He counted his change. He craved a smoke, and he had just enough money for a pack, but he bought a lotto ticket for a dollar, and then he was too short for cigarettes. Scratched a loser. He had enough for a burger but went into that sum for another dollar.

As he touched the ticket, he could feel it in his fingers. He set his money clip on the counter and flattened it with the heel of his hand and slipped the ticket into it along with nothing but his driver's license.

Two bucks in his grip. He bought two tix. Scratched a loser, and the second one hit for ten. "There we go. See that?"

"You want it in tickets?"

"Just a pack of Camel straights. No. You got Luckies? It's Luckies from now on. And those Twinkies. And I'll get a can of Sprite or something. You got matches?"

"Now you're back to zero."

He cracked the deck and lit up and raised a hand in farewell.

"Are you walking?"

Luntz said, "I guess I'll hitchhike."

"You better clean up first."

"Yeah? Where's the washroom?"

She shook her head. "The whole back of your pants is like you been rolling in dirt. You better find some deep water."

"Where's the river?"

"Right over there a half a mile."

"Is it cold?"

"It's cold. But it won't kill you."

picador.com

blog
videos
interviews
extracts